3 1628 00034 8616
AVON PUBLIC LIBRARY
P9-ELS-094

WITHDRAWN

Mama, Let's Dance

Mama, Let's Dance

A Novel by *Patricia Hermes*

Little, Brown and Company
Boston Toronto London

11/91

For Maria Modugno and Joan Elizabeth Goodman

First Edition

Library of Congress Cataloging-in-Publication Data

Hermes, Patricia.
Mama, let's dance : a novel / by Patricia Hermes.
p. cm.
Summary: Abandoned by their mother after the death of their father, three youngsters are determined to keep their situation a secret so that the authorities will not split them up and send them to foster homes.
ISBN 0-316-35861-4
[1. Family problems — Fiction. 2. Brothers and sisters — Fiction.]
I. Title.
PZ7.H4317Mam 1991
[Fic] — dc20 91-11988

10 9 8 7 6 5 4 3 2 1

MV-NY

Published simultaneously in Canada
by Little, Brown & Company (Canada) Limited

Printed in the United States of America

Mama, Let's Dance

Chapter 1

Whenever I would dream about her, I'd dream of her dancing. She'd be whirling into the kitchen, looking younger than Callie even, spinning round and laughing. Her arms would be held wide, inviting Callie or me to dance. Callie would run into her arms, and they'd laugh together as though they were both Callie's age, not mother and daughter. They'd keep up whirling and dancing like that, like dancers in the movies in their pretty dresses, but that's all they'd do — Mama wouldn't talk, and Callie wouldn't ask where Mama'd been or anything. And Ariel, he'd just stand and watch the way he always used to do.

Me, I'm not much of a dancer, but in my head I'd be writing the music for them, composing it, the way I've done ever since I first learned to read music in school. I often hear music welling up inside me, new music that no one else has written before.

After a while, the dream would fade, the way a picture fades from a movie screen, with them getting faint, like shadows. I'd look for the place where they'd been, the way you watch the place on the screen, but they'd be gone. That would usually be when I'd wake up. Sometimes I'd find I was sitting up in bed with my arms stretched out toward them and that feeling in my throat as though I was about to cry, "Please come home, Mama. We need you." But no sound would come out.

Instead, I'd lie down again and I'd feel all shaky. How could she come back laughing and dancing like that, as though what she did wasn't wrong at all? She hadn't changed any, not even in my dreams.

After a while I'd fall asleep, safe from the dream because it never seemed to come back twice in one night. But the following night it would be back. Mama would be whirling, laughing, reaching for us. And it would always be Callie who'd go into her arms.

But that was only in my night dreams. In my daydreams, I pictured her dead. She'd be in a ditch somewhere, her car turned over and she'd be crushed beneath it. Or else she'd had one of those spells she used to have when she said she felt as though she were about to faint, or "fade," as she called it. At those times, she'd call us to her and she'd hold onto us tight, Callie and Ariel and me. In my daydream, I would make her *really* fade away, and I wouldn't stop her fading.

Callie was just the opposite. In Callie's daydreams,

Mama would be alive, while in her night dreams, Mama would be dead. Callie didn't call them daydreams, though. She'd just say she *knows* Mama's coming back. Once, she even stayed home from school, watching at the kitchen door the whole day long, because she was so sure that was the day Mama would come back. And even when Mama had been gone for six weeks, with not one single word, still Callie believed that she was coming home.

At night, though, when Callie slept, then I knew that for her, too, our mama was dead. I knew because I'd wake up and hear Callie crying in her sleep. I'd get up and sit on the side of her bed, and I'd talk to her until she was wide awake and the sad dream was gone. Because now that Mama had left us just the way Papa did, taking care of Callie was my job. Ariel had other things to do for us, but Callie, she was my job.

It had been my job for all those weeks. When Mama first left, I gave her one month. I didn't say so to Callie, but I thought that at the end of a month, Mama'd be back. Everybody needs a month off now and then. I used to wake up, thinking I heard her tiptoeing around, as though she had just come home and was getting ready for bed, just regular-like. But that was mostly wishes, and I was old enough to know that wishes are not the same thing as the truth. So the month had come and gone, and we were in the second month, and I knew then that she was gone for good.

It was hard, though, because if people had known Mama was gone, I didn't know what they'd do. They might have tried to take Callie away from me. And Callie was all I had, Callie and Ariel. Ariel's older and quiet and a bother sometimes, so bossy to us. But I guess that's just the way boys are, especially ones who are almost grown. I love Ariel, too, but Callie had always been the one I loved most.

I hadn't talked to Callie about what might happen if people knew. But Ariel and I talked about it just once. I asked him, after Mama had been gone for a few days, if we should tell anyone, some grown-up, maybe someone like Amarius, my friend. But Ariel said just plain no. If anyone knew, Ariel said, even Amarius, then he might talk. If he talked, then the county people might find out, and then, Ariel said, who knows what might happen?

"What do you mean, 'who knows?'" I said.

Ariel looked at me and shrugged.

"Ariel! What do you mean?"

He tossed his head so hard that his sandy hair flew away from his forehead and eyes, giving him sort of a surprised look for a minute. "You know," he said. "You know just as well as me."

"Say it," I said.

He gave me one of his looks, long and hard, his gray eyes cold as a winter lake. "Why do you always want everything said?" he demanded.

I thought of saying, "For the same reason you don't want them said." But he looked sad behind his cold eyes, so I didn't. It was true, though. I had always needed things spoken out, because — just because I did. Hidden things, not talked about, cause trouble. I had learned that one from Mama. She had so many secrets, things that made her run away in the night. But I guess that's just how it worked out for me. For Ariel it's just the opposite — he deals with things by not talking.

He kept looking at me, that angry look still there, but a scared look growing behind his eyes. He looked away then. "Because they might take you away," he said softly, "you and Callie, too, just like they did that other time, after Papa left. Separate all of us in foster homes or something. You remember."

I did. Lord, yes.

"I won't tell," I said. "Don't worry."

"Not anyone. Not even Amarius," Ariel said.

"Not anyone. Not even Amarius," I said. But then I thought, and I said, "What if someone finds out by accident? What about like school? If a teacher calls?"

"Nobody'll call. Why would they?"

"They might."

"They won't. If they do, just say Mama's out."

"I'll think of something," I said.

Ariel picked at a hole in his jeans. "Sorry you have to lie," he said.

I was glad he wasn't looking, because it was hard not to smile. Ariel's so nice and honest. He has always said his prayers every night and morning on his knees — I've seen him through his doorway. He reads his Bible, too, even though nobody makes him. But he didn't know the truth about me, that if telling lies were the only way to keep us together, I'd have lied to God himself. Because if we weren't together, especially me and Callie, I thought I'd die.

Some people, like Anna Tilley, my best friend in school, she's always saying things like, "I'll just die!" all the time. Mostly that's if Billy Hancock doesn't look at her, or if she doesn't get a new dress. But that's "cheap words," like my friend Amarius would say. But when I say I thought I'd die without Callie, I mean something different.

I read once, in a book about a tribe of Pygmies, that if one of the Pygmies got sick, the others would say that the Pygmy was dead. And if he got *very* sick, they'd say he was absolutely and completely dead. But when the Pygmy really died, then they'd say that he was dead forever. That's how I felt about Callie — if anything happened to her I'd be dead forever.

Since that day, we all took extra care to look neat and have our homework done and all so that no one would ask about us or call or anything. And since Ariel was working then after school, there was enough money for us to eat. Ariel didn't talk about money much, and when I'd ask, he'd tell me not to worry, that it would work out, we were going to be all right.

"There's food money," he said once. "And you know yourself there's no rent."

I did know. It was something Mama had said lots of

times, that it was the only good thing that Papa had left her, a house that was all paid up. I used to wonder, though, why she didn't include Ariel and Callie and me as something good.

Ariel worked so hard that I worried about him. Like one night: I was still awake when he came home from his job at the gas station. My bedroom's right next to the kitchen, and my door was open. He didn't know I was awake, watching him. I saw him come in, plop down on the kitchen chair, open up a can of soda, open his algebra book — and fall asleep. He fell fast asleep, without even turning one single page. He just put his head on his book on the table and went to sleep, right there.

I knew how important Ariel's grades were to him — he's gotten straight A's since kindergarten — so I got up and went to the kitchen to wake him up. But looking at him in the chair there, he looked peaceful for the first time in a while. So I just got the quilt from the sofa and put it over him. He didn't wake up even then. But the next morning, when I got up, I could see that his bed had been slept in, even though he was already gone to school.

I used to wonder sometimes if Papa would ever come back. That was long ago, after Papa first ran off but before we heard about the mining accident where he went and got himself killed. Before that happened, though, I used to daydream about what I would say to him and what he would say to me when he did come home. I learned fast, though, not to talk about it. I mentioned it to Mama once, and she almost took my head off. She turned to me fast, her hands on her hips, fingers hidden under her apron, elbows flared out.

"What makes you think he'll be back?" she demanded, her eyes little slits in her thin face. She was always telling me how pretty she used to be, but she didn't look pretty then, glaring at me like that.

I'd been sick with measles, and I'd been lying in bed hurting and itching and bored with nothing to do. When you're hurting, you feel mean sometimes. All I could think was that if Papa were there, he'd have brought something for me, things to make me feel better. Maybe a doll whose hair I could comb, or at least something to make me stop hurting and itching. Best yet, though, I knew that Papa could make me laugh. I remembered only a few things about him, but I did remember that he was always laughing and he made me laugh with him.

He made Mama laugh, too. I remember him and Mama laughing and whispering on the porch on summer nights, Mama's laugh bright as though she was a child. But that had been long ago, when I was just a child, too.

But that day, with Mama glaring at me, I'd only shrugged.

"Why?" she insisted. "Why do you think he'll be back?" Her eyes weren't squinted up any longer, and she was looking at me with this very still look, like she was hoping for something.

I didn't know what she was hoping for, and truth was, I didn't really think he *would* come back. I just wished it. So I said, "I want him to come back because he wouldn't be mean like you."

For a minute, her face got dark and cloudy, and I thought I was in big trouble. But she just came and sat on the bed and brushed my hair away from my face. "Feels that bad?" she said quietly.

I nodded. It did feel bad, the measles and the loneliness. Her being gentle like that made it worse, because it made me feel sad for her. I discovered something that day — when you're sick and hurting yourself, it feels worse to hurt for someone else than it does at other times.

But I noticed something else that day. I think it had been there all along if I'd been watching carefully, but I'd been missing it: Mama thought he'd come back, too, even after all those years. I began to notice that she would sometimes stand perfectly still, listening. There might be a footstep on the porch, maybe just Ariel outside playing, or a whistle from off in the field, even a bird whistle. For a moment, she'd go still as a statue, and then her hands would go to her hair in a quick, nervous way. But it wasn't just nerves. She was trying to pretty herself up, to pat her hair into place. I'd see something else then, a *look* come to her face, a practiced, pretty kind of wide-eyed look, like she was waiting for him to come in, waiting to show him she was still the pretty person he'd left so long ago.

Then, after a while, when no one came to the door, she'd go to the window and lift the curtain and look out.

I'd hear her sigh, and her shoulders would kind of collapse forward, and she'd fold her arms, as though hunching to protect her chest where her heart was. After a while, she'd straighten up. But almost always after that, she wouldn't turn back to face me for a little while, even if I spoke to her. It was as though she needed time to fix her face, to put on a different look, one we could all stand to live with.

But all of this was long ago — when I was just six or seven or so. Papa was gone for good, and now Mama was gone, too, and we'd just have to make do somehow. We'd have to until Mama decided to come home to us. And if she never decided she needed to do that, then Ariel and Callie and I would manage somehow. But for now our biggest job was to make sure that nobody knew, not school, not friends, not anyone, that the three of us were all alone.

Chapter 2

I had given Mama one whole month to come home. And then I made it six weeks. If she wasn't home by then, I'd stop thinking about her anymore. I was good at that. I could tell myself what to think and what not to think, and I could do it most of the time. I didn't know why Mama left, and her letter didn't help because it didn't make any sense, but I couldn't change that now. She was gone, and Callie and Ariel and me were just going to go on, and everything would be fine in a little while.

In the middle of that second month, I put my plan to work. No more thinking, no more hoping. She was gone. And as Mama herself would have said, that's all there is to it.

Sometimes it got hard, though, because things kept

happening. Like in class one day: I had decided I'd make up some lies for Mama so nobody would know she's missing. I had practiced how I'd talk about how she's home washing curtains and doing spring house-cleaning just like all the other mamas in town, so no one would think anything was different. Then I remembered. Everybody knows Mama's never done a lick of housework in her life. So I settled on a story about her having a cold, nothing big because then all the women would come to the house bringing casseroles covered with glass tops, but mostly, they'd be coming to spy. Everybody's been curious about us ever since Papa left. That's what Mama says anyway, what Mama used to say.

So I had this story all ready in case anyone asked, snoopy Ellie Mae, especially. Ellie Mae's whole name is Ellie Mae Rooks, and her mama's name is Ell*a* Mae Rooks, and I never heard anything so dumb in my life. Why would you name a child with a name almost just like her mama? It seems to me they should know the child would turn out just like the mama, which is exactly what happened in this case. I'd think that before someone did that, they'd want to be mighty sure that they'd *want* another human being to turn out like themselves. Anyway, I don't know if they ever thought about it, but if you ask me, it was a *big* mistake, but of course, nobody did ask me. I wasn't even born yet, as Ellie Mae loves to tell me. And they sure turned out alike, not just their personalities but the way they look: horrid red hair on top of barrel-shaped bodies.

That morning, Ellie Mae didn't ask about Mama, but

she sure enough noticed something. It was early morning before class began, and she smiled at me when I came in, her nose wrinkled up like she smelled pig.

"That's a right nice hair clip you got on," she said.

I waited. Ellie Mae never gave a compliment for no reason.

"When's the last time you washed your hair?" she asked.

"What business is it of yours?" I said.

Her face was still scrunched up in that pig-smelling kind of smile. "Looks like last year," she said. She laughed, her laugh sounding exactly like a pig snort. With her nostrils flared out like that, she even looked piggy.

When had I washed my hair last? That was something we hadn't paid attention to since Mama left, regular days for hair washing.

I started to put my hand to my hair, then stopped myself, but I could tell that I was blushing.

"Doesn't your mama make you wash your hair?" she said.

"Mama said I can't wash it, not when I have —"

"Hush!" Ellie Mae blurted out. "Why you just hush!" Her face went as red as if she'd been out picking beans in the noon sun, and she looked around, checking to see if anyone had heard me.

Behind me, I heard Anna Tilley giggling.

Ellie Mae was just furious looking. She bent close to me. "Your mama better tell you about talking about it out loud," she said.

She turned away and went back to her desk, going sideways to fit down the aisle between the desks.

I turned to Anna Tilley. "What's the matter with her?" I asked.

"She thinks you have *it*," Anna whispered. "Let her think."

It was our word for when you get your period. I didn't have mine now, never had, and at the rate I was going, probably never would. I was one of the last ones in the whole class, but maybe just because I'm the youngest. I had just turned eleven, and all the others were twelve already, and everyone knows why that is. It's because Mama couldn't wait to get us kids in school, and she made such a fuss that the school people took us. Actually, I'm smart, so it didn't matter much. It was harder on Callie, though. She'd always been smart, too, but she was just a baby in a lot of other ways. She had just turned seven the day Mama left — but already Callie was finishing up third grade.

I sat down at my desk and bent close to Anna Tilley. "All I meant was Mama said I can't wash my hair when I have a cold," I said. "Why can't I wash my hair when I have *it*?"

Anna Tilley giggled again. "You can. That's just an old wives' tale. She's just copying her mama, and you know her mama doesn't know anything."

True. But her mama considers herself the unofficial town leader, preacher, and general, overall God. Nobody asked her; she just elected herself. Although come to think of it, maybe God did the same thing. But now her mama was sure to hear from Ellie Mae that I had *it* and not only that, but that I was talking about *it*. And it would be just like her to call and tell Mama what I should and shouldn't say about *it*.

I looked at Ellie Mae sitting there in the front of the classroom, and if it wasn't that her chest is a little smaller and her hips not quite as wide — although they're getting there, I swear — then you'd think that Ell*a* Mae, the mama, was right there in class. It's downright spooky, I mean it.

I'll never turn out like my mama. I'll never run away and leave my kids, making them have to cover up for me and pretend that everything's the same — hair washing and all.

Ellie Mae didn't say anything more to me that day, snubbing me, as if I cared. But I was glad when school was over, and I planned on waiting by the phone at home, just in case her mama called. I'd have some story ready about Mama.

After school I walked home with Margaret and Beth Ellen and Anna Tilley. (I don't know why, but I can't ever think of Anna Tilley as just plain Anna. I always think of her with both her names.) It was a bright, pretty spring afternoon, with the sun beating down so hot you could really believe that summer was coming on, and we walked slowly, our faces turned up to the sun.

My house lies way out from town and away from the rest of the houses, way out along a dirt road that runs back into the fields. After a mile or so, the road thins out so it's hardly a road at all, just a narrow path that goes on for another mile, and then ends at our house at the very foot of the mountain. I'd always walk with them to the place where my road branches off. There's a creek that crosses the road right there — Narrow Passage Creek it's called — and sometimes in spring rains, you have to wade across the water waist deep, unless you know the hidden places where there are boulders to step on, places that we know but that hardly anyone else knows. It makes the road seem most secret, as though it belongs just to us.

When we came to Narrow Passage Creek, Margaret and Beth Ellen and Anna Tilley said, "So long," the way they always did, and I said, "So long," the way I always did. They left, and I crossed the creek and started up the road alone.

Suddenly, my heart started thumping like crazy. Because up ahead of me was this little girl I had not seen before. That in itself was awful strange, not just because I know everybody in town, but because I didn't know of any visitors around. But even more, our house is so close to the mountain, so far from town, that nobody comes along our road unless they're coming to see us. I was about to hurry, to catch up and keep whoever it was from finding out about Mama. But something about the girl made me want to hold back, till I was sure what to do. She was familiar, like she was . . . But it couldn't be. Callie?

No, she was too thin for Callie, much, much thinner. Yet the dress was Callie's dress.

She had an old doll in one arm and an umbrella in the

other, although the sun was shining and had been shining all day. She was dragging the umbrella along in the dirt, dragging it and singing.

It *was* Callie.

She sang softly, her voice clear and sweet, like children on those Christmas records, but the song she made was awful sad, even sadder than the ones I make up in my head. It was so sad it made me shiver. Then she began to dance. Right there in the middle of the dusty road she danced, holding that red umbrella and the doll close to her the way you'd hold someone in a dance. The way Mama held her in my dreams.

I ducked behind a tree, not wanting her to see me. I knew she'd stop dancing in a minute, open her eyes and feel downright dumb being caught dancing like that. I stayed still as a mountain lion behind that tree, but Callie didn't stop. She danced on and on, holding her umbrella, singing louder now, songs that were a mixture of nursery rhymes and Christmas carols, and even ads from the radio. But somehow, coming from her mouth, all of them were awful sad.

After a while, I got mad. This was dumb. She had no business acting crazy in the middle of the road like that. What if anyone saw her? She had no business looking so sad either.

I stepped out from behind my tree.

"Callie!" I said.

She opened her eyes and laughed. "Hi, Mary Belle," she said. She didn't seem even a little bit embarrassed. She came to me and took my arm, tucking hers through mine, the umbrella and doll in her other arm. She laughed up at me. "You look pretty," she said. "Wish I had long hair like yours."

I pulled my arm free. "What're you dancing for in the middle of the road?" I said. "Are you plain crazy?"

"We always dance, Mama and me. And Mama and *you* even sometimes," she said.

"That was long ago! It's over!"

She looked away, but before she did, I saw the hurt in her eyes.

But I went on. "What if anyone saw you?"

She blinked up at me then, her gray eyes wide and serious. "Who would see me?"

She was right about that. Nobody came along this road, nobody but me and Ariel. But that wasn't the point.

"Come on," I said. "We're going home. And you're going to eat something, too."

I must have sounded awful mad, because Callie got real anxious looking, the way she would when people raised their voices.

"I do eat!" she said.

"Well, you're going to eat more," I said.

I knew I sounded mad. I didn't mean to. It was just that I felt guilty. She was so thin! How come I hadn't noticed before? She'd probably not been eating right ever since Mama left, and I'd been too dumb to notice. Suddenly then, I noticed other things, how her pretty blond hair looked flat, no shine at all, and her freckles stood out sharp against her pale skin. I wondered if anyone at school had noticed, anyone like Ellie Mae. If she did, there was sure to be a call from her mama about that, too. But more than that even, I was mad at Callie for acting so weird like that. Dancing with an umbrella and a doll and singing sad songs!

"Yeah," I said. "Well, you're going to eat a lot. And I'm going to watch that you do."

She shrugged. "Okay."

"Have you really been eating?" I asked her.

She nodded.

"Honest?"

She sighed. "You see me. I eat with you!"

She was right. We did eat supper together. But I guess the truth was I hadn't paid any attention at all to what she ate.

We were both quiet then, walking up the road. It was a long road, hot and dusty and pitted with ruts, with not a single house or even a barn or shack along the way. Unshaded by any trees, the combination of the heat and dust could sometimes take your breath away. Not that it was so difficult that I didn't have enough breath left for talking, but it was a good excuse to be quiet so I could think. How could I have been so stupid not to notice what Callie ate? I washed her clothes and ironed them and packed her lunch and helped her with her homework. But I had forgotten to watch her eat — and forgotten to wash our hair. Well, I'd just have to fatten up Callie, that was all. Make sure she ate. I'd watch to be sure she did, too. I'd also wash my hair tonight, and hers, too.

"Mary Belle?" Callie said.

"Hmm?"

There was a long pause.

"What?" I said.

"Nothing. Never mind," she answered.

"Callie, that is *so* irritating!"

"I forgot what I was going to say."

"You did not."

She seemed to be thinking that over. "Mary Belle?" she whispered. "Do you think she'll come back?"

It was the first time she had ever asked, the first time she had even hinted that Mama might not come back.

She was looking right at me, her wide gray eyes clear and direct. She didn't look afraid. She didn't look sad. She didn't look anything. Just wide gray eyes, waiting for an answer.

No sense in her hoping for what wouldn't happen. So I said, "No. She's not coming back."

Callie nodded. She took a shaky breath like a sigh, but she didn't begin to cry or anything. She just made this weird sound, as though she were trying to say something but words were stuck in her throat. Then after a bit she nodded again, and then she did the oddest thing. She folded her arms across her chest, hunching her shoulders forward, as if to protect the place where her heart was. Just like Mama used to do.

Chapter 3

It was the following Saturday that I found this note lying under Callie's bed, written in her little-kid handwriting, all careful letters, with lots of erasing and mistakes in spelling. It said, "I know this."

Underneath, it listed these things all down in a row, as if she were making out a shopping list of things that she knew. This is what it said:

I am seven years old.
I can write in cursiv.
I am in the blue reading grup.
God is mad at me.
Ariel is mad at me.
Ariel is mad at Mary Belle too.
I am trying hard to be good.

I can tell time.
Mama is coming back.

How could she be so dumb! God wasn't mad at her. Neither was Ariel. And Mama was *not* coming back. I already *told* her that. I thought she'd understood that at last.

"Callie!" I yelled.

I went to the back door. I knew she'd gone out in the yard, and I found her there, sitting on the grass, leaning against the trunk of the red-bud tree. She was playing with her doll Lisa, smoothing Lisa's hair down over and over again, singing to her softly.

I waved the note and yelled to her again. "Callie!"

She looked up and her eyes went to the note in my hand.

"A letter?" she said, and then she added, "*Mama?*"

At least, I thought she said, "Mama." Her mouth formed the word, but no sound came out.

I swear she stopped breathing then. Her face went so quiet and so white and her hand that had been patting the doll stopped right still in midair.

I looked away.

"Mary Belle?" she said, her voice rising.

"Don't have to yell. I hear you," I said.

She made me so mad! Why hadn't she put *me* on that list of people mad at her?

"Is it a letter?" she said. "Is it?"

I stuffed the note in my pocket. I couldn't tell her that her list was stupid and wrong, not now.

"No, it's not a letter! It's just a shopping list," I said.

"Oh."

She took a big, wobbly breath and bent over Lisa again. After a minute, I could see that her breathing went back to normal. I knew, though, what she was thinking.

"Want to play something?" I said.

She carefully put the doll down and got up. She came over to me. "We could play dancing," she said.

"No!"

"You never want to dance anymore," she said. Her lip came out in a pout.

"And that's all you ever want to do!" I answered.

She opened her mouth to answer. I know what she was going to say — that when Mama was there they danced. But she knew better. Her mouth just snapped shut.

After a minute, she said, "Want to play house?"

I was still mad at her, so I said, "We *are* playing house, Callie," I said. "For real. You think I *like* fixing lunches and washing dishes and braiding your hair and —"

I saw the look on her face and stopped.

She turned away and folded her arms.

"All right, all right," I said. "I'll play house if you want."

"You don't stay mad long," she said.

She should know!

We went back in the house then, and Callie gave directions for playing.

"You be the mother," she said. "I'll be a baby. You can teach me to bake cookies with clay."

While I got out the clay and some pans, she talked to me in baby talk. She was pretty good at it, too, maybe because it hadn't been all that long since she'd really been a baby.

After just a little while, Callie said, "Can we go to the store now? Or the gas station and see Ariel?"

I knew why: she was tired of the game. Playing house is only fun when it *is* a game.

I hesitated. I hated going to town on Saturday. It wouldn't be good to meet people and have them ask after Mama.

But I was just as bored as Callie. And there was money in the sugar jar, and we did need stuff. Callie and I could shop and make a good supper for Ariel when he got home from work today. It had been a long time since we'd had anything but macaroni and cheese or hot dogs. Maybe we could get chicken and make mashed potatoes and get Mallomars for dessert.

I looked at the clock. It wasn't twelve o'clock yet. I had a better idea! We wouldn't have to wait for supper. We could make sandwiches for Ariel and buy fruit — grapes for Ariel — he loves grapes. I'd buy him tons of them, and I'd buy chocolate milk and bring it to him at the gas station. All three of us could have a picnic together!

"Let's do it," I said.

"Can Miss Mannie come, too?" she asked.

"As if we could stop her," I said, laughing.

Miss Mannie is our dog, and nobody knows how she

got that fancy name, especially since there is nothing mannerly or polite about her at all. She just showed up one day out on the back steps, this collar around her neck with a name tag that said Miss Mannie — dirty and hungry and so tired she could hardly stand, as if she had walked miles and miles to find us. We looked and looked for who owned her, but she wasn't anybody's, not anybody in town anyway or we'd have known. Maybe she'd been let out of a car by somebody on the highway north. Lots of people do that, get a summer dog and when they go back north, they just leave it behind. Or maybe she'd belonged to one of those civil rights workers who'd been around that year. Anyway, Miss Mannie acted as though she'd heard that this was a good place for a dog and so that's why she came. She's been with us ever since, years now. We've been calling her Miss Mannie all this time.

Callie went outside to get a rope for Miss Mannie, and I went to the refrigerator.

There was practically nothing in there but eggs and milk and a jar of apple butter and one of sweet pickles — homemade ones, but not made by Mama. Mama didn't hold with making things like pickles and apple butter like the rest of the mamas around town. But she didn't mind taking the jars when the ladies came visiting. Showing off, they were, Mama always said, but she took the jars anyway.

There was nothing there for sandwiches, so I decided we'd take the loaf of bread and buy lunch meat when

"How are we going to find her if we don't tell?" Callie said. She had turned her back to me, but I could tell that she was close to tears.

"Callie. She doesn't *want* to be found. Can't you get that through your head? She left. She doesn't *want* to come back."

Callie began digging the toe of one shoe in the pebbles between the tracks, raising little clouds of white, ashy dust.

I could feel my heart begin to pound hard. She had to know it was important not to tell. She had to know that they might take us away, separate us. But I didn't want to scare her either. She was just a little kid.

"Callie," I said. "You can't. It's important. Trust me. You've got to promise me."

Callie shook her head, still not looking at me.

Miss Mannie laid her big red head against Callie's side and whined more pitifully than before.

I swear, that dog thinks she is a person.

"Callie," I said. "Just today don't tell, okay? We'll talk about it more later, okay?"

She turned around, her arms folded. She hadn't started to cry, but she had that stubborn look she gets. "When?"

"Tonight." I'd figure out something to say. I'd talk it over with Ariel. "I'll tell you why tonight. Okay?"

She still had that stubborn look, but she said, "Okay." She turned away again. "I already told," she said.

"You *told*?"

"I told."

I grabbed her arm, but she jerked away like before.

"Who?" I said. "Who'd you tell?"

She stood facing away from me, her head tilted up to look at the sky, her arms still folded.

"Somebody."

"Callie, I swear —"

"Miss Mannie," she said. "So there. I told Miss Mannie."

For a minute, I didn't know whether to laugh or slap her. She told Miss Mannie!

Miss Mannie began to bark, as though hearing her name gave her the right to get in on this conversation.

"See?" Callie said. "She knows."

That only made Miss Mannie bark louder. She began circling round and round us, barking and wagging her big old tail, her tongue hanging out like she was laughing.

"Shush!" I told her. "Hush! Quit!"

But Miss Mannie kept it up, barking and lolling her tongue at us. And Callie began laughing.

Then, after a while, I started laughing, too. I couldn't help it. Callie was laughing, and our secret was safe. It was only us, Callie and Ariel and me and an old red dog, only us who knew that our Mama was gone.

Chapter 4

At first I thought Ariel wasn't happy to see us, the nervous way I saw him looking around as we came up to the garage. But then he came and joined us under the tree that shaded the side of the garage, and he smiled when he saw the lunch, especially the grapes. There were some overturned metal drums there and an old picnic table without benches, but the drums worked pretty good as benches.

We ate the bologna sandwiches, and Ariel ate three huge bunches of grapes. He didn't say much. He never does, but I can pretty much tell his moods anyway. And he was happy to have us there, I could tell. When we were almost finished, he began packing up the leftovers.

"So, what have you two been up to all day?" he asked.

"I was playing with Lisa," Callie said. "I washed her hair."

"Hope you didn't get soap in her eyes," Ariel said.

"I didn't. I'm careful."

"Good thing," Ariel said. He was grinning.

"Well, dolls have feelings, too," Callie said.

"I know!" Ariel said. "That's why I said, 'Hope you didn't get soap in her eyes.'"

"Oh," Callie said. "I thought you were teasing."

"Me?" Ariel said. He was laughing.

"Yes!" Callie said, and she was laughing, too.

She moved in closer to Ariel and put her head against his arm.

His beautiful gray eyes lit up, and I realized I hardly ever saw Ariel laugh anymore. He had changed so since Mama left. He had always been quiet — got extra quiet after Papa ran off — but now he was even more so than before. He was always either at work or at the kitchen table with his books. He was still getting all A's, too, although how he did it with work and all, I couldn't figure. Yet now, for a moment, he seemed happy, bent close to Callie, his tall body folded over, face close to hers.

He smiled down at her, then looked at me over her head. "And you? What'd you do today?" he asked.

"Laundry," I said. I wanted to keep him smiling, so I added the only other thing I could think of. "I did your other jeans."

"You're a good kid," he said.

"She is," Callie said.

I looked at the top of Callie's head. Should I say what I was thinking in front of her? I hated to worry her, or to worry Ariel, but I was so worried myself. "Money?" I said quietly. "Do we have more?"

Ariel frowned, and I was sorry that I'd brought it up. "More? More than what?" he asked.

"There's practically nothing left in the sugar jar. Not 'practically.' There is nothing!"

"I get paid tonight."

"Yes, but —"

"Stop worrying, we'll be all right." He stood up, moving Callie's head gently from his arm. He looked at the little clock on the fake bell tower over the garage. "I got to go now. What are you two going to do this afternoon? What's up?"

I gave Miss Mannie the crusts of my sandwich. How could he say not to worry? What if there was no money for food?

"The sky," Callie said. "The moon. Stars. The sun. Heaven . . ."

She would have gone on, but Ariel put a hand on her arm.

She put her own hand over his and held on to it, grinning up at him.

"We're going home," I said.

"You coming, too?" Callie asked Ariel.

"Later," he said.

"Come now," Callie said. "Miss Mannie wants you to."

Ariel smiled at her. "How do you know what Miss Mannie wants?"

"She told me," Callie said seriously.

"Well, I can't come yet, Miss Mannie," Ariel said. He leaned down and patted Miss Mannie's head. "Later, when I'm finished work."

Then he stood up and patted Callie's head, both of them the same way, as though Callie was a little dog, too. But his hand stayed on Callie's head for just a minute.

She reached up and put her hand over his again, just as she had before.

For just a second, watching them like that, I felt a little jealous. I wished sometimes that I was little enough to have somebody do things like that to me. But of course, I didn't really. I would have hated it if Ariel patted me on the head as if I were a dog or a little baby or something.

Ariel was looking at me, his eyebrows raised, something like a little smile in his eyes. I knew immediately that he guessed what I was thinking. I felt my face get hot.

"Let's go, Callie," I said. I grabbed the lunch bag and started toward the street.

"Wait," Ariel said.

He caught up to me, reached into the pocket of his jeans, took out a dollar bill, and handed it to me.

"Get some ice cream on the way home," he said.

The dollar was damp, probably from his sweat.

"Ice cream!" Callie squealed. "Yay! Ice cream!"

Miss Mannie began to bark.

Callie grabbed Miss Mannie's front paws and began dancing with her, pulling Miss Mannie up so that she was on two feet. "Ice cream, ice cream, ice cream!" Callie chanted while Miss Mannie kept barking.

I couldn't take the money. Even though we hadn't had ice cream in longer than any of us could remember, not even when Mama was still at home, I couldn't take it because I knew why Ariel was giving it to me. He was doing it because he felt sorry for me, because he knew what I'd been thinking.

I shook my head and stuck the money back in his hand.

"Take it," I said.

"*You* take it," he said. He shoved the money back at me again.

I pushed it back at him.

"Will you stop it?" he said. "What's the matter with you?"

"The matter?" I said, angrily. "How can we buy ice cream? What do you think we're going to do when the money's all gone?"

I shouldn't have said that. I didn't mean for it to come out the way it did either. It was just that I felt weird inside.

Ariel folded the dollar bill, reached over, and put the bill in the pocket of my jeans. Very quietly, he said, "Just get some ice cream."

He turned and went back to the gas pumps. But as he went by, he patted me briefly on the head.

Callie let Miss Mannie drop back to four feet. "We can afford it, Mary Belle," she said. "Ariel's working."

I nodded. But I had to turn away. I was going to cry. For the first time since Mama had left, I was going to cry.

Chapter 5

That night, I got Callie to agree not to tell about Mama by saying that if Mama knew we were looking for her she might hide even more. Callie nodded gravely, as though she understood. But I didn't know for how long she'd agree to this.

At school next day, I watched out for Callie, trying to see if she looked happy or if she was moping, making people — *teachers* — notice something was wrong. But she sure acted okay, maybe because she was with her friends.

I was standing on the playground talking to Anna Tilley when Callie came racing by me, pursued by Naomi Lynn and about ten other little kids in a pack, all of them with their hands outstretched.

Callie was laughing, and when she saw me, she practically slammed herself into my arms, breathless. "Save me, Mary Belle!" she yelled. "Save me! Monsters!"

All the other little kids crowded around, wiggling their fingers and reaching for her.

"Wiggly-finger monsters!" she yelled.

"Go away, wiggly-finger monsters," I said. "Leave Callie alone."

Callie pulled my face down close to hers and wound her fingers in my hair. Then she turned back to face her pursuers. "Stop!" she said, and she raised her hand. "I am your queen. Stop!"

"Yes, Your Highness!" one kid said.

"Yes, Your Honor!" another kid said.

All the rest took up the chant — "Yes, Your Honor. Yes, Your Highness" — all of them bowing before Callie.

And then the whole pack took off again, running and laughing and chasing each other.

If only Callie could stay that happy, I thought. If only she could.

It was twilight a few days later, and I was sitting on the porch steps, rereading Mama's letter. Callie was already asleep, and Ariel wasn't home from work yet. It was the only time I could read Mama's letter, when no one was around. I tried to understand it. Over and over again I tried. It wasn't long and the words weren't hard to understand, but I had the feeling that there was something there that I was missing, that if I just understood what she really meant, then I'd understand why she left the way she did.

But even though I read and reread, I still couldn't see through to the meaning.

The letter said this:

Dear children:

You mean everything in the world to me. That's why I've stayed all these years. Now you're old enough to take care of yourselves and each other. I know you can do it and I know you will.

Take special care of Callie.

The electric bill and the phone are paid up. Keep the lights off — it saves money. The house is free and clear. We paid cash for it, the whole thing in cash. The deed's in the middle drawer of the living room desk. There's money in the sugar jar for food, as much as I can afford to leave. It should last a while. You'll make do, I know. You can get jobs after school, and in the summer there's always farm work.

Ever,
Mama

P.S. There's always the county people if you really get stuck.

I folded the letter. It was beginning to come apart along the creases, and I handled it carefully when I put it into my pocket.

I stood up, thinking as I had about a thousand times before, Why did she say Callie needed special care? Had she noticed before she left how skinny Callie was? Or did she just mean because Callie's so young?

It must have been that, that Callie's the youngest, because she didn't say anything about me or Ariel.

But the part I really couldn't understand was that part about us meaning "everything in the world" to her. And the word *Ever.*

If only we had someone, some relatives like other people had, aunts or cousins. But Mama had no brothers or sisters, and her parents died when I was just a baby. And Papa's family came from way over the other side of the mountains, and none of them ever spoke a word to Papa after he married Mama — when both of them were younger than Ariel is now.

I was so scared of the county people finding out. When Papa first left, and Mama spent so much time just sitting on the porch, staring and not moving, it was so scary. She didn't come in to feed us or to put us to bed or anything.

At first it was fun. Ariel and I stayed up late and played outside in the dark, and one night, Callie even fell asleep under the porch. But then we began to feel scared. We tried to take care of Mama, to bring her in the house and put her to bed. But after we got her to stand up and we tried to lead her into the house, she just shook her head and sat back down. The only time she moved was to go in to the bathroom. She'd stay in there a real long while, then come back to the porch and sit again, watching the road again as if she were sure he'd come up it any minute.

The worst part was about Callie. She was just a baby, not even two yet, and both Ariel and I tried to take care of her. But Callie just screamed and hollered something awful if Ariel even came near her, and so that left only me to care for her. But I was only about five or six years old, and I didn't know what to do either.

I remember that when she slept under the porch that night, she got covered with bug bites, probably from sand fleas. She broke out in big red hives, and she cried and cried, and I put something on the bites, baby powder, I think. It probably didn't help at all, but I didn't know what else to use.

I tried to feed her, too. When we ran out of stuff in the refrigerator, I tried to open a can of pork and beans. But I had trouble opening the can, and when finally I got it partway open and went to scoop out the beans, I got cut real bad. Then when I tried to feed it to Callie, she kept shaking her head no and spitting it out and yelling.

By then I was crying, too, because my hand was bleeding pretty hard and it hurt. Ariel, when he saw what happened, plunked Callie in the playpen, wrapped up my hand in a towel, and took me to Dr. Brody. We walked a long way to get there — I still remember that, the whole two miles on the dirt road and then another half mile through town. I remember, too, how red the towel was by the time we got there and how scared I was. I got stitches, the first time I had them, and the last. I got a lollipop, a red one, and Dr. Brody let me put on his tie while he put the stitches in. It was a red and green plaid tie. The stitches hurt, though. And I still have the scar.

It was a little while after that, maybe the same day, that a car showed up in the yard. It was county people from the Welfare Board, and they took us away — not Ariel, just Callie and me. It was only for a few days — I don't know just how many, but it felt like forever. I remember the car ride with the Welfare lady, and how I rode with Callie sitting on my lap, hugging her close, and how she wasn't crying anymore. And then that awful house they took me to, and how they wouldn't leave Callie there. That's when I started to cry really hard, and that made Callie cry again, too. I begged them to let Callie stay with me, but the lady whose house it was said she couldn't take care of two kids, that one was enough. I said that I'd take care of Callie myself, that she wouldn't have to do anything. But nobody listened to me, and they took Callie away anyway.

I don't know till this day why they let us go back to Mama, except that Mama began feeding us after that. I also know that the county lady came back every day for a while and talked to Mama. I think that that by itself helped Mama, maybe just having another lady to talk to. Still, for a long time after, Mama would sit and just stare. But we made do. We did. We even began to have fun after a while, especially when Mama started to take dance lessons and to teach dancing to us.

Mama and Ariel danced, and sometimes Callie and me. Although usually I didn't dance. I just watched them twirling around, and while they danced, I wrote music in my head for them. Later, in my room, I wrote the music down in a little copy book that Miss Danforth, the school music teacher, gave to me. The pages of the book were ruled, with lines and spaces for music. Miss Danforth thought I was smart, the way I had learned to read music so fast for such a little kid, and she found an old recorder that some kid didn't want anymore and gave it to me, to play the songs I wrote. The recorder wasn't the best, but it was better than nothing. But oh, how I dreamed of one day owning a piano. Once, when Ariel learned what I was doing, he made Mama turn off the radio, and he had me sing some of my songs. Mama wouldn't dance to my songs, though. She said they weren't dancing songs. Ariel and Callie liked them though.

Mama decided she'd learn to dance so well she could be a professional dancer. She said she'd make it some day, right up on a stage, like in the movies. I had to say she was an awfully good dancer. She seemed to just float in some dances, as if her feet were barely touching the floor.

So, as Mama got better, for weeks and weeks, especially in the summer, we laughed and danced, sometimes on the porch in the moonlight. Callie and I danced together a little, and Mama and Ariel danced a lot. Ariel got to be the man who led the dances, just as though he were the papa, until he said one day that he was too old for that. That's when Callie became Mama's partner. For some reason, Mama didn't invite me to dance very much.

So we got by. We did. And we'd do it again. If only . . .

I began to think that maybe I understood what Mama felt like now. I hadn't dreamed about Papa coming back in years, not since I was a little kid, but I dreamed about him now, even though I knew he was gone for good.

It was almost dark by then. I'd been staying out of doors as much as possible lately, sitting on the porch and keeping the lights off, just like Mama said.

I got up off the steps and walked to the edge of the porch, looking out over the fields. There were some acres there that belonged to us, but Mama never planted them after Papa left. The fields stretched away, melting into hills that swelled gently upward to Black Brother and Hairy Bear mountains far off in the distance. It was pretty out there in the twilight, and I could hear birds calling and see swallows swooping over the fields, getting a last snack of bugs before bed. There must have been plenty of bugs there in the old dead cornstalks and weeds and hay.

The only thing Mama ever planted was a small garden she called the kitchen garden. It was way out back by the barn, and she kept it up every year — used to keep it up. She and Ariel had put up a fence around it to keep out the rabbits and deer, and she'd planted tomatoes and cucumbers and lettuces and cabbages and peppers and carrots and onions and herbs. But there was nothing planted there this year.

And then I realized something. Mama hadn't planted anything this spring! Then she must have been been planning on leaving for a very long time.

And she never told.

I sat on the railing, just looking, thinking, listening.

Tree frogs were calling loudly now, making a wild, seesawing kind of racket, so loud that it was hard to believe it all came from such little throats. I guessed I should have felt lonely there, Mama gone and us alone, not even another house in sight. But truth was, at least for the moment, I wasn't lonely. I loved this place, the quiet, the hills and deer, the mountains in the distance. Even this house, with its sloping porch and silvered, faded walls, the paint gone, I loved it all. The moon had come up, a small, silver crescent, an old moon, bright over the hills. One minute it wasn't there and the next, it was high in the sky. Maybe there really was a God, one who could lift a moon like that. Ariel thought so, anyway.

It was then, looking out over the fields, that I saw someone walking in the yard in the moonlight.

Mama? Mama!

No. A man.

Who?

A ghost.

Not a ghost!

A man, a tall man, walking stiff, as if he were old.

Someone who knew us, someone looking for Mama?

My heart began clattering against my ribs.

I turned to hurry inside. The lights were off. Whoever it was, he'd think we weren't home, were in town.

Why would we be in town on a school night?

Stay on the porch then. Tell him . . . What would I tell him? Mama was sleeping. She'd gone to bed early with headache. She was . . .

But it couldn't have been anyone looking for Mama, because he would have come straight toward the house.

Instead, whoever it was was walking around inside the fence, inside the kitchen garden.

Why? And who was it?

I went to the edge of the porch.

"Who's there?" I called out. I tried to sound normal, but my voice was shaky.

"That you, Miz Loma?"

Amarius! Amarius! I hadn't seen him all spring.

"No," I answered. "It's me, Mary Belle. Is that you, Amarius?"

"It's me, Miz Ma'y Belle."

I jumped off the porch and ran toward the back garden.

I hadn't seen Amarius in ages. He used to work for us, helping with the haying. I've always liked him specially well, and when I was little, I told everybody that he was my best friend. I think the first thing I loved about him was his name. When I was little, I thought his name was Amaryllis, like the flower. It was Mama who told me it wasn't Amaryllis at all. "It's Amar-ee-us," she said. "Silly!"

I felt shy about making that mistake, but I still thought being named after a flower was a good thing, so to myself, for a long time, I kept calling him Amaryllis in my head. He'd always talked to me as if I were a regular grown-up, even when I was just a little kid. We'd talk about everything, but his favorite subject seemed to be God. Other times he would tell me about what it was like to be a slave, even though he couldn't have known that himself since he'd have to be much more than a hundred years old for that. But he said he knew what it was like anyway, and I always imagined that maybe he had lived other lives a long time ago.

He lives in a small gray house way back out of town, about a mile from us, with his niece or maybe it's his grandniece, Miss Dearly Aikens. Callie'd always loved Miss Dearly, was always trying to copy the bright, pretty head scarves Miss Dearly wears. Whenever Callie saw Miss Dearly in town, Callie took her hand and clung to her as if she and Miss Dearly were best friends. People say Amarius and Miss Dearly have so much money — they even have a piano! — that neither of them needs to work. I don't know if that's true, though, about them having so much money. Amarius is always looking for jobs it seems to me. But the thing I like best about Amarius is that he's always been nice to us, even after Papa left, when some of the people in town started acting like we were plain trash.

The garden gate was open, and Amarius was inside poking a stick at the ground.

I leaned over the fence. "Amarius!" I said. "Where have you been? I haven't seen you in so long."

Amarius pushed his straw hat toward the back of his head. He smiled at me, his teeth showing white against his skin. His skin is so black it looks almost blue at times. It's stretched tight against his cheekbones, and there are no wrinkles at all. I can't tell how old he is, but people say he's about ninety. I don't think he could be. The only way I can tell he's even a little bit old is that he walks slowly and his legs are a little bowed. And that he's always talking about "goin' home." By that he means dying.

"You're looking good, Miz Ma'y Belle," he said.

"Thank you," I said. "You, too."

He made a funny sound, deep in his throat, sort of a quiet kind of laugh, a nice sound.

"Don't matter how I look," he said. "Be meeting the Lord soon, and He don't care how I look."

"Stop talking like that," I said, laughing. "You're not dying soon, and you know it."

He laughed again, that low, quiet sound, and said, "You're late planting this year, Miz Ma'y Belle. Your mama should know that."

"Yeah. Well . . . maybe we won't plant."

Amarius looked straight at me. His eyes are deep set, almost hidden under his brow bone, and they were staring out at me as if I had just said a swear. "No!" he said. "How come?"

Ariel said I should not tell even Amarius. He worked for too many people. If he knew, others might find out, too. Although I didn't think he'd tell. Still, I had promised.

"No reason. Don't want to, I guess."

He didn't answer for a while. Then he said, "It's going to be a fine growing season. Plenty of sun and plenty of rain, and all the rain at night."

"How do you know that?" I asked.

I didn't say it in a sarcastic or ugly way — I meant it as a real question. Amarius always seems to know things people can't possibly know. And he's right lots of times, too, as if maybe he does really talk to God.

"I know," is all he said. And then he added, "I could be by in the morning to help you."

If he did, he'd wonder why Mama wasn't out in the garden working with us. And even though having a garden would help save money, I didn't have any seeds. But even more important, there was no money to pay Amarius.

"No. No, thanks," I said.

Amarius came out of the garden and closed the gate quietly behind him.

He stood for a moment, looking up at the sky. Then he tipped his hat to me and turned away.

"'Night, Miz Ma'y Belle," he said softly. "Sleep sweet."

"'Night, Amarius," I said.

Chapter 6

We settled into a kind of routine after that, Callie and Ariel and me. We did our work, went to school, came home, and stuck together. Another week went by, and I even stopped worrying so much about people finding out. I began to think that maybe people didn't really care that much what other people did, not as much as I thought, anyway. But best yet, Callie had stopped talking about Mama so much, and maybe even she was forgetting a little, because she sure was happier. One reason for the happiness was something that happened at school.

Every year there's a big fair on the last day of school, the May Fair. Everyone comes, not just kids and their parents, but everyone in town. Projects that we've been working on all year are put out for people to admire, like our dyed T-shirts and our map of the town with all the historical places marked out. There are rides and games and races and a parade, and lots of things to eat that all the mamas make. One girl is chosen to lead the events, to be the May Queen. (It's a pretty dumb name considering that the fair isn't held until June first, but that's what she's called.)

The May Queen rides on the royal float at the very front of the parade. She wears a white dress and a crown and throws candies to the other kids. The float is only Mr. McCardle's hay wagon covered with chicken wire stuffed with Kleenex made to look like flowers, but it's pretty anyway. There's also a Queen's Court that has two handmaids and two maids of honor (more dumb names), and the court gets to ride on the float with the queen. Not only that, but the queen gets to pick the girls for her court. Of course, everyone wants to be May Queen.

Yet nobody knows how the person is picked. It's a secret, something the school people decide. Sometimes they say they choose the best pupil, and sometimes they say it's the one who's improved the most over the year. Nobody ever knows for sure. But I do know this: sometimes they really mess up and pick a mean and ugly May Queen, like the year they picked Ellie Mae.

But this year, they were smart.

It was the day that they were to announce the May Queen that Anna Tilley came to me at recess. She grabbed me by both hands and twirled me around.

"Guess what?" she said.

"What?" I answered.

She stopped twirling and pulled me close to her. "Bet anything Callie's going to be May Queen."

"Callie!" I said. "Our Callie?"

"Shush! Not so loud. No one's supposed to know."

"Are you sure? How'd you find out?" I whispered.

"I heard Miss Callahan and the principal, Mr. Richie, talking. They were talking about how good a student Callie was and how many friends she has, and then Mr. Richie said, 'She deserves it, sweet little thing. I bet her mama will be proud.' And then Miss Callahan, she said something, but I couldn't hear, and Mr. Richie, he laughed. But I bet anything that's what they were talking about."

"Wow! This is so great. And Callie needs it, too."

"Needs it?" Anna Tilley said.

"Well, not needs it, but you know . . ."

"What?"

What?

I just looked at Anna Tilley, my best friend.

She has a little, squinched-up face, close-together eyes, pointy nose, not really pretty at all. Actually, she looks a little bit like a gerbil or a mouse. But she's my best friend since I was four, and suddenly, with her looking at me so close like that, I wanted so much to tell her.

"What?" she said again.

It was the closest I came to telling anyone about Mama. I knew I could trust Anna Tilley. But if I told her, there was no telling how she might just let it slip out, not meaning to or anything.

"Nothing," I said.

Anna Tilley scrunched up her face at me. "You're lying, and I know it," she said laughing. "And I know what's the matter, too."

"Do not. 'Cause there *is* nothing the matter."

"Ha!" she said. "You wish it was you who was May Queen. That's all right. I wish it was me, too." She took my arm and laid her head against it for a minute. "But I'm not pretty. They'd never pick me. But if it can't be you or me, then I'm glad it's Callie."

"I'm glad, too," I said. And I surely meant that. I also meant that I was glad that Anna didn't suspect what was really the matter. "And there's nothing wrong with the way you look," I added, "so stop saying that."

She just smiled.

And Anna Tilley was right. They announced about Callie that afternoon, right after lunchtime: Callie, our Callie, Queen of the May.

Later that day, when Callie and I were walking home together, she was so excited, she could hardly stand herself.

"Me, Mary Belle!" she kept saying. "Me! They picked me, May Queen! Like a real queen!"

She danced all around me. She held her arms out as though she were a ballet dancer, and she twirled in circles. Then she began to run round and round me, her arms still flung out, but looking more as though she were playing at being an airplane than a ballet dancer.

I caught her as she twirled by, and we hugged. "My sister, May Queen!" I said. "I'm so proud of you!"

"Me, me, me!" she sang. "Callie, May Queen!"

I did wish for a minute that they'd chosen me, just like Anna Tilley had said. But it was all right. Callie was really the best choice.

Callie started whirling again, running round and round me the way Miss Mannie did.

"You know what else, Mary Belle?" she said, stopping so short that I almost tripped over her. "I get to pick the Queen's Court."

"Who're you picking?"

"Naomi Lynn," she said.

Naomi Lynn was Callie's best friend, a girl almost as sweet as Callie herself.

"That's good. She happy?"

"Yup. And you know who else?"

"Who?"

"You!" she said, and she threw her arms around me again.

"Me?" I was embarrassed. She shouldn't choose me. Other May Queens always chose their court from girls in their own class.

"It's supposed to be kids from your class," I said, untangling myself from her.

She made a face. "Says who?"

"Everybody."

"Don't you want to?" she asked.

I looked away. I didn't want to hurt her feelings, but I really *didn't* want to. People would talk, and they'd say that it was just because she was my sister. They might even think that I talked her into doing it.

"Not that," I said. "It's just that's the way you do it — you've got to pick girls in your class."

"But I want you!"

"I'm glad," I said. "But I don't think you should. Choose girls from your class. Isn't there anyone who wants to?"

"Everybody," she said, real disgusted-like. "If I pick one, the others will get mad. And I don't know how to pick."

"You'll think of something," I said. "Besides, it's good for them to wait while you decide. Makes you the most popular girl in the class."

She made a face.

After a minute, she looked up at me. "Mary Belle?" she said, shyly. "I'm supposed to have a white dress."

There wasn't any money for a dress. In fact, Callie needed shoes badly, much more than she needed a dress, and I didn't know what we'd do about that either. "I'll figure it out," I said.

"How?"

"Don't worry about it."

"But I am worried. See, if I don't have a dress, they might —"

"You'll have a dress." I didn't know how, but she would. Even if I had to steal one. "Leave it to me," I said.

We had just come up on the porch. We were still outside, but we could hear that the phone was ringing. The phone! Our phone hardly ever rings.

Callie gave me a wide-eyed look, almost frightened. Then, as if she were escaping from a swarm of yellow jackets that was suddenly chasing her, she flung open the screen door and flew into the house. I saw her grab the phone from the table inside the door. From the look she gave me before she ran in, I knew just what she was thinking. She hadn't forgotten Mama at all.

But it was only someone from Callie's class, two someones. I heard her call them Isabelle and Cindy Sue, and they seemed to be taking turns begging Callie to let them be part of the Queen's Court. I heard Callie say something about not needing them to be her best friends forever, that she just needed time to think for a while. Then she put down the phone, looking as sad as she did when Mama first left.

I pretended not to notice. I don't know why I did that. Unless maybe because when the phone rang, I wondered, too, if it was Mama calling at last.

Callie went to our room without saying anything, and I went directly to Mama's room.

If Mama was gone, I was at least going to use whatever she had left. I opened her closet. Most of her clothes she'd taken with her, but there were a few things left, hanging every which way off the hangers. There was a red-and-green-striped summer dress with a jacket. I remembered Mama buying it, and remembered, too, that I'd never seen her wear it. There were some sweaters with the elbows worn out, and a long khaki wool coat, a man's army coat, pockmarked with moth holes.

When had it ever been cold enough in North Carolina to need a coat like this? I wondered where Mama had gotten the coat and why she had kept it in her closet.

Then I saw what I had hoped to see, crammed way in the back corner: a white dancing dress, hanging by two thin straps from a bent wire hanger. I pulled it out. It was lacy and maybe too fancy for a May Queen, and was more yellowish than white. But it was soft, and it made a nice swishy sound when I shook it. I held it up to me. It came all the way to my feet. I could shorten it. I didn't know much about sewing, but I could learn. And maybe with a good washing, the dress would come real white.

I took the dress to the kitchen and laid it on a chair. I'd wash it tonight, and tomorrow Callie could try it on. Then I'd figure out how to fix it, cut and shape and sew and all. I felt better. We had a dress. Mama had been good for something.

That night, after Callie was in bed and read to, I went outside to sit on the porch. Sitting outside at dusk had gotten to be the happiest time of my day. I'd watch the herons fly home from the pond downstream, watch swallows dip and glide, watch bats swoop from the old dead tree. The swallows made me think of music I once heard on the radio, with twin violins swooping up and down. Sometimes deer would come timidly down from the mountain to graze at the very edge of the field, flicking their white tails. One doe always stood with her head up, watching, as though she had chosen to guard the rest. I'd sit out there till the sun set. And then I'd keep on sitting even after dark, listening to the night rain fall — because Amarius had been right and rain was only falling at night this spring. It fell from clouds that hung low on the mountain, and I could hear the rush of streams as they swelled with rain and spilled over the rocks on their way down the mountain.

I thought about the phone call that afternoon. I guess I hadn't really expected it to be Mama. I had even stopped dreaming of her. Weird, I used to wish sometimes she'd go away but I never wished she'd go for good. Mama was so restless, always moving, dancing, always wanting to be somewhere else, and sometimes her restlessness made me nervous, as if it might become catching.

Now, I felt guilty for those thoughts, yet I loved the peace here, that night even more peaceful than usual, crickets chirping, cicadas singing their high-pitched song, swallows swooping, and the stars coming on, one at a time, like lights. Tree frogs were calling, too, in a shrieking chorus from tree to tree, each one singing a different part, some high, some low, blending together as though they were a people chorus. I wondered what they were saying to one another. I pretended they were children frogs after school. They were calling, "Come to my house; no, you come to mine. Come to my house; no, you come to mine." Mama had never let me have a friend over, not even once. Not even Anna Tilley, my best friend.

I was daydreaming like that, listening and looking out over the fields and the marsh, when I again saw someone walking about in the garden.

I stood up. "Amarius?" I called.

There was no answer. I came down from the porch. "Amarius?" I called again.

I started toward the garden. It would be fun to talk to Amarius again, even if he did tell me again that he was going home to God.

I went on across the field, peering through the dusk toward the garden. But now I didn't see anyone anymore. Whoever had been there was gone. Or had I just imagined it?

I felt sad inside me. I hadn't realized how lonely I had become suddenly, how much I wanted to talk to someone.

I wondered why he left without speaking to me. Unless it wasn't Amarius. But who else would it have been?

I went on more slowly, till I was right by the garden fence. And I stopped still, my heart hammering wildly in my chest.

The garden had been planted. Row after row had been hoed. There were baby lettuces, their tiny green curls of leaves already coming up. There were mounded-up rows that were beans, with sprouts sticking up from them, and there were rows of radishes, already about two inches tall. Long poles had been set by the far fence, ready for climbing peas or beans or vines.

Amarius! It must have been him. But I didn't *want*

his help. I didn't need him. But even more, I couldn't pay him. Besides, it wasn't any of his business that we had no garden.

He'd been working for a long time, too, because the garden was not only planted but free of weeds, and the fence had even been mended, I could see that.

My heart was beating crazily. This meant he'd guessed about Mama. He must have, and that's why he did this while I was away, so I wouldn't feel I had to pay him. But if he was here during the day, that meant he *knew* that Mama was gone.

Would he tell? No. At least I didn't think so. He never told anyone's business to anyone else. If you asked about something he thought wasn't any of your business, he always said, "The Almighty knows all, and He ain't tellin'." And that was all the information you got.

I turned, looking for him, but there was no one there. Or was he hiding in the shadows, ready to come out when I was gone, to do some more work that I didn't ask for? Some more work that I couldn't pay for? Mama was gone. That was our business. What right did he have to poke into our lives and, and . . .

We didn't need anything!

"Stupid old man!" I said into the darkness. "Stupid, stupid, stupid. Who *asked* you to nose in here?"

Talk about stupid. I started in to cry.

I opened the gate and went inside the fence. Suddenly, I began doing something I didn't mean to do, and then, once started, I couldn't stop. I began with the row of radishes closest to me. I began yanking them out of the ground. They had the tiniest roots, just baby radishes, not ready for eating or soup or anything. I went all the way along the row, yanking them out, throwing them over the fence. Then I started on the next row.

Lettuces. One at a time, I began yanking. Pull it up, throw it over the fence, pull it up, throw it over, up and over, up and over. By then I was crying so hard, I could hardly see what I was doing.

Dumb! Stupid! I should have been happy. We'd have food now, and that would save us money and trips to town. But I pulled them out, crying, wiping my face with the bottom of my shirt, and yanking plants as fast as I could. He had no right knowing we were alone. He had no right doing stuff for us that we didn't need, that we didn't ask for. That we couldn't pay for.

I sat down on the ground by the fence. Dumb, dumb, dumb. It was just a kitchen garden.

I don't know how long I sat there. The stars were fully out by then, coming down almost to the horizon. The tree frogs were quieter, and the deer had gone back up into the mountains. And Amarius? Was he back in the woods, watching?

After a while, I blew my nose in my shirt hem, got up, and went back to the house. I went in without turning on any lights and went straight to my room.

The moon's light came through the window, lying across Callie's bed. She lay on her side, breathing softly, smiling in her sleep, clutching her ragged cloth dog, not even knowing she was lying in a square of moonlight.

I got undressed and dropped my clothes beside the

bed. I didn't brush my teeth or wash my face or scrub the dirt from under my fingernails. I just pulled on the shirt that I slept in, got into bed, and pulled up the covers.

I lay there on my back, waiting for sleep.

I don't know how long I lay there watching the square of moonlight move across the room. I didn't think anything, just lay absolutely still. I knew if I moved I'd start thinking. I heard Ariel come in. I saw the kitchen light come on, heard the refrigerator door open and then close. The light went out. Water ran in the bathroom. I heard Ariel peeing, the toilet flushed. I heard Ariel's footsteps, and then — then I heard him whistling. He must have had a good night at work, because he whistled quietly as he went down the hall to his room. I heard him close his door, his bed squeak. And then be still.

And still I lay awake.

I must have fallen asleep sometime, though, because I was awakened when I heard an owl call.

The moonlight had shifted, so that the light was now clinging to the very edge of the window sill. The owl sang again, and I wondered if it was looking down on Amarius, working in the garden, putting back the plants I had thrown aside. But I didn't get up to look.

Chapter 7

Two days after I tore up all the planting, I came out to sit on the porch in the evening, after seeing that Callie was settled and sleeping. Callie had been restless, and it had taken a while to get her settled. She said her throat hurt when she lay down. Now, how can a throat hurt when you lie down and not hurt when you sit up is what I want to know. But Callie said it did, so I just propped her up with pillows and then sat with her till she felt sleepy. So it was extra late and almost completely dark by the time I came out to the porch.

My eyes had not yet adjusted to the night, so I didn't see Amarius standing by the porch steps, as still as though he were one of the hollyhocks that grow there.

When he spoke up, I thought I'd die he scared me so.

"Evening, Miz Ma'y Belle," he said.

"Oh, Amarius!" I put a hand to my throat. "You scared me!"

He didn't say "sorry" or act sorry. He only looked at me across the porch railing, his eyes hidden in shadow.

"What?" I said, my heart still thudding hard in my chest. "What are you doing here?"

"Come to see your mama."

"Mama? Why?"

"Now, what kind of question is that?"

"Well, she's not here. Not now. I mean, she is but she . . . she said she didn't want to see anybody."

"She feeling poorly?" Amarius asked. Sly-like. As if he knew.

But I just said, "Yes. She is. Very poorly."

"'Cause somebody tore up her garden?"

I didn't answer that. There was no law that said I had to answer that.

Amarius sat down on the porch step, the bottom one, his back to me. Was he going to wait, wait till Mama got better, till she came out?

Nosy old man! Why did I ever think he was my friend?

But I couldn't just send him away. Besides, I had a feeling he wouldn't go even if I told him to.

"Mama doesn't have a garden," I said finally.

To my surprise, he laughed.

"Not anymore, she doesn't," he said. He lifted one hand then and pointed.

Through the dusk, I could just make out the outlines of a herd of deer that had come out of the woods and stood at the edge of our field. Quietly, they spread across the field, grazing, heads down, tails flicking.

I looked for the one who was on guard and found him — or her. There is always one who guards, whose job it is to protect the others, to warn them of danger.

But I did not do good at my job. I must have messed up somehow, because Amarius, he knew. And he didn't beat around the bush, as my mama would have said.

"Your mama isn't here," Amarius said. "I know. And she's not been here for a long time. Where is she?"

I looked toward the deer, the one whose job it was to guard. Her head was high, her ears seeming huge, wide and open to the danger in the wind.

She gave a signal — she must have given a signal, for suddenly all the deer moved together, as if in a dance. Their white tails flicking, they cleared the rail fence and then were gone, heading back toward Hairy Bear Mountain.

"I don't know where she is," I said slowly. Oddly, instead of feeling scared when the words came out, I suddenly felt relieved, maybe just at having spoken the words at long last.

"When?" Amarius asked. "When'd she go?"

I knew exactly when.

Sunday night March thirteenth, or early in the morning of the fourteenth. I found the note when I woke up, March fourteenth in the morning. The morning of Callie's seventh birthday.

"Two months ago," I said. "Almost two months."

"Leaving her babies," Amarius said quietly.

"We're not babies!" I said.

"You're *her* babies, though," he said. He turned to me.

I was still standing on the porch above him. He watched me a while, then nodded once, as though he'd seen something he'd expected to see.

I came down from the porch. I did not sit on the steps beside him but sat instead on the railing where it fans out at the bottom, making a wide flat place.

"I always knew they'd do this. Or something just as stupid," Amarius said.

"Who? Do what? Leave, you mean?"

"Your mama and papa. I always knew they'd leave their babies like they were no more 'n wild pups. Just like that!" He clicked his tongue against his teeth.

"You couldn't know that," I said. "I didn't even know it."

"I've known them a lot longer than you have. How are you all making out?"

"We're okay. We're eating."

"Bills? Rent? How about money?"

"Ariel works," I said. "And there's only two bills, electric and phone. I paid them myself. I took the money to the electric company and the phone company in town, and I got receipts."

I was proud of that. I knew that I ought to get a receipt. It was proof that we paid in case some person came and turned off our lights to leave us in the dark because we didn't pay our bill. I had put the receipts in the desk drawer along with the book of accounts that I had been keeping. I was proud of that, too, that account book. Ever since that day of the picnic, when I got so scared about money and food, I'd been keeping an account book. Ariel gives me all his money except he keeps his own school lunch money, and I knew now how we spent each cent we get.

Amarius sat quietly for a long time, thinking I guess. He is always slow to speak, and that was all right. It just takes him time to think things out, to decide just what was right to say. But was he thinking now about telling somebody about us being alone? Would he feel he had to?

He wouldn't. I didn't think he would. Still . . .

"Are you going to tell?" I asked.

He didn't answer for a minute. And then he said, "Just Miss Dearly. She'll know what to do." Miss Dearly, His niece.

"But she works for the county. She'll —"

"You can trust Miss Dearly. She won't tell."

"She . . . If anyone knew they might take us away. Like last time, the county people might separate us."

He didn't answer.

I sat and waited.

After the longest time, Amarius said, "Your mama, she'll be back."

My heart raced, skipped. Amarius knew her, for a long time he'd known her. And he said she'd be back!

"Sooner or later, she'll be back," he said.

Later, he'd said.

"Meanwhile, we've got to get you food and some care. Your sister and that brother and you."

"Care? We care for each other."

We do. Oh, Lord, yes we do.

Amarius hauled himself to his feet. There were clicking noises as he rose, as if he weren't made of flesh and bones but was made out of an old potato sack with dried-up sticks inside that slid against each other as he moved.

I stood up with him, hoping he wouldn't go yet. Now that he knew, now that there was finally someone to talk to about it, I did not want to let him go. Not that I had much to say to him, but I did not have to hide, to pretend.

"You going home?" I asked.

"To the garden first," he said. "See what I need to do next."

"I'll help you," I said.

"Mighty dark," he said.

"If you can see, then I can see," I said.

He laughed. "I'm used to it. I see in the dark good as anything. My God and me, we like the dark."

I thought about my bedroom, the nights I lay awake. I could see in the dark, too, I thought. But I didn't like what it was I saw in the dark, the things that moved across my ceiling, the things that followed me who does not guard well enough. But I didn't think that Amarius meant that kind of seeing.

"Want me to get a flashlight?" I asked.

"I'll be back tomorrow," Amarius said. "We'll work after school."

"I'll help you," I said. "Me and Callie both."

I couldn't say I was sorry for pulling up the garden, for some reason I couldn't say it. But I was sorry. And if I helped to plant, that would make it better.

I felt so much better suddenly, happy almost. Amarius knew, and he wouldn't tell. And he'd help us. He could help us take care until Mama came home.

Amarius picked up a long, heavy-looking stick that had been resting by the step. He set one end gently on the ground. I hadn't noticed it before, and it was the first time I'd seen Amarius use a cane.

But then he lifted the stick to his shoulder, and I saw that it was not a stick or cane at all. It was a gun for hunting.

"You be careful," I said. "Don't you trip in the dark."

"Haven't blown my head off yet," he said, "or my foot neither." He shifted the gun to his shoulder. "Like to blow away some other heads, though. Imagine, leaving your children like they were so many pups."

And then I said something, said it without at all planning to say it. "I think about hurting her," I said. "Breaking her ankle, so she can't dance again."

"You should," Amarius said softly. "Sure to God, you should."

And that's when I realized something — that even though he was agreeing with me, still I realized you cannot tell someone what they should or should not feel. You should only forgive them for it.

Chapter 8

Next day at school, I felt different, relieved almost. Amarius knew our secret, and it was safe with him.

It must have shown, how I felt, because Anna Tilley said to me, "You look happy today."

"I do?"

"Yeah. *Very* happy." She said it as if she meant something important by it.

I just shrugged.

"Bet I know why," she said. "But I don't know who."

"Why?" I said. I knew she couldn't know why *or* who.

"B-O-Y-S," she said, spelling it out. "Which one?"

"You're silly." I said.

"Tell!" she said. "Come on. We're best friends. I'll tell you mine."

"I'd tell," I said, "but there isn't one."

"Ha!" she said. "I'll find out. I'll watch."

I just laughed. "So go ahead, watch. But when I pick one out, I'll tell you. And it won't be creepy-face over there."

I nodded at Robert Wright, who was watching me from across the playground. Robert Wright was *always* watching me.

Anna Tilley made a face at him, then turned back to me. "It's some boy. I know."

I just smiled. I wondered what she'd say if I told her she was partly right. It was a boy — a man, really. Amarius, but not for the reason she thought. It was just that he knew our secret now, shared our secret — and it was safe with him.

That afternoon after school, Callie and I joined Amarius in the garden. I had told Callie that Amarius knew and that I also knew he wouldn't tell. But I had to remind Callie that she couldn't tell anyone else, not anyone at all.

It wasn't easy working in the garden. The sun was hot, and even though the garden was pretty big, it seemed small with so many of us in it. Each time I bent to plant or pull a weed, I bumped butts with Callie or Amarius and once even with Miss Mannie. Callie had insisted that Miss Mannie be with us, as if we did not have enough of a crowd in the tiny garden without a dog to keep us company. But eventually, with all three of us working, and in spite of Miss Mannie interfering, we had the garden planted — well, replanted.

When it was done, we walked up to the house —

slowly and quietly, dragging, we were so hot. Miss Mannie was hot, too — you could tell. Her tongue lolled out, and she panted hard, her sides heaving in and out.

Back at the house, Amarius sat in the shade on the porch and Callie sat beside him. I went in the house to get water for all of us. I got the old yellow glass pitcher that we have had just about forever, filled it with water and ice, and got three glasses. I also got a bowl for Miss Mannie. I put ice cubes in her bowl because she loves that. She pushes the cubes around with her tongue, then laps them into her mouth, and you can hear as she crunches them between her strong yellow teeth.

I put everything on a tray and brought it out to the porch.

Callie had moved closer to Amarius and was showing him her favorite stones. She practically always had some stones in her pocket — smooth and flat, or smooth and round, or smooth and shaped like dice. Always smooth. She'd gather them when we'd walk up into the hills, or sometimes from the place where Narrow Passage Creek crosses the road.

The one she held out to Amarius was very small, shaped like a boomerang. Amarius took it in his slim fingers, gray now with garden dust, and he was turning it over to inspect it.

He nodded, then dropped it back into her outstretched palm.

"You want it?" Callie asked. "You can have it if you want. I got others."

Amarius took the tiny stone back from her. "Thank

you kindly," he said. He slid it deep into the pocket of his baggy black pants.

I handed round the glasses and poured the water, and we all drank. Amarius drank slowly and steadily. I've never seen anyone drink like that — never put the glass down from his lips, just drank slowly, slowly, slowly till the whole thing was gone.

Miss Mannie emptied her bowl, making a lot of noise and raising her head after every few laps to show the water and saliva dripping off her muzzle. Yuck.

Amarius wiped his mouth with his sleeve. "What've you all been eating?" he asked suddenly.

Callie laughed and made a face. "Stuff. Mary Belle's a awful cook."

"I am not! I cook fine. Better than you!"

I felt like saying, if I'm such an awful cook why don't you try doing it for a change? But I didn't. She was too young to use the stove, at least for a regular meal she was, although I did let her fry eggs sometimes.

"I remember when I first started cooking," Amarius said laughing softly. "Lord, I was a mess!"

"Mary Belle's a mess, too," Callie said.

"I am not, Callie! Now, stop it!"

"My first time at the stove, I must have been thirty years old." He looked at us, grinning slyly. "Women did all the cooking in those days, but I didn't have no woman then, so one day I just up and decided to cook for myself. I cooked up a mess of greens and some ham. First time!" He laughed softly and slapped his thigh. "Oh, Lordy!"

"What?" Callie asked. "Was it awful?"

"Awful? Lord, it was so awful even the coons wouldn't touch it when I threw it away!"

Callie laughed and screwed her eyes up tight. I could picture what she was seeing in her imagination, her eyes screwed up like that. "So what'd you do? What'd you eat?" She inched closer to Amarius.

I came down and sat on the wide part of the railing where I'd sat the night before, looking up at them.

"I took myself to the store and bought a cookbook, and I learned how to cook. And I can cook!" He slapped his thigh again.

Mama has a cookbook, I thought. I could learn to cook new things. But it wasn't the new things that was wrong with my cooking. It was money. We had eaten hot dogs and beans more nights than I wanted to remember. That and macaroni and cheese out of a box. But macaroni and cheese was cheap — buy two boxes and you got two free when it was on sale — and all you need to add is milk. Four boxes lasted us two nights.

"How about if I bring you something tonight?" Amarius asked.

"Like what?" Callie said.

"Ham. Collards. Or I could fry you up some chickens."

"Yay! Fried chicken!" Callie clapped her hands.

"Callie!" I said.

"What?"

I frowned hard at her. We didn't need help, didn't need neighbors to feed us!

"He asked!" Callie said. "Didn't you, Amarius?"

He nodded. "I did. And I make good fried chicken, too. Yes'm I do."

I stood up and started collecting glasses. "No, thank you," I said.

"But Mary Belle!" Callie grabbed at my shirt as I went by. "He offered! And I love fried chicken. You never make it. And —"

"And we're having pea soup with hot dogs in it," I said. I pulled free from her hand. "I already started it. I started the peas last night. They've been soaking overnight, ever since you went to bed."

"I *hate* pea soup!" Callie said. She folded her arms and made a fierce pouting face, her bottom lip jutting out, her eyebrows drawn together.

"You do not! You like it, and you know it!"

Amarius was watching me. "It'd give me pleasure to do it," he said.

I picked up Miss Mannie's bowl from the porch floor and put it on the tray with the glasses. "Pea soup," I said. "Pea soup is what we're having tonight. Thanks, anyway."

"Well, I won't eat it," Callie said softly.

I went in the house and slammed the screen door.

"You'll eat it," Amarius said. "You will. Remember, it isn't an easy time for Miz Ma'y Belle."

"Well, why's she have to be so grumpy all the time?" Callie said.

"Not an easy time for her," I heard Amarius say again, softly this time. "Not a tall."

I slammed the inside door, too.

What did they know, either of them? They didn't know what it was like to worry about every single cent and what would happen next or if they'd have anything to eat.

I sat down at the desk in the living room and took the little notebook from the middle drawer. Could we afford to buy our own chicken, to make fried chicken for ourselves?

I went over our accounts, the electricity, food, other things. There wasn't much listed under "Other Things." But soon there would have to be. Callie needed shoes. We needed screening for the back door where the flies were getting in through the holes as if they owned the place. And Miss Mannie needed flea powder or a flea collar — she was itching herself like crazy all day long. Even at night, you could hear her foot thumping against the ground as she was scratching, hear her teeth gnawing herself. But worst, Ariel's two pairs of jeans were getting real worn out and holey. I bet jeans cost a lot of money. And our radio, the only thing that brings music to the house, was beginning to make crackling sounds so that some days we couldn't hear anything on it at all. Most families in town had TVs now, but I knew we'd never get a TV.

Next to money we spent was money we got. All of it came from Ariel's work at the gas station. But of what he got, practically all of it was going back out for food.

Still, school would be out on Friday, and I could get work on one of the farms. Or maybe I could baby-sit somebody's kids? But then who would care for Callie?

Well, she wasn't exactly a baby. She could stay alone.

I pictured her sitting alone under the red-bud tree, smoothing Lisa's hair, only a doll to talk to. I knew then I could not leave her. But maybe she could come to work with me wherever I went?

I turned to the back of the book. I had put away five dollars, hadn't even listed it in the book. It was in an envelope clipped to the inside of the book for an emergency.

Was this an emergency — fried chicken for Callie? It couldn't be. Or could it? I thought then that maybe emergencies are not what I used to think they were, not since Mama left.

I heard the door open and close behind me.

Callie.

"What?" I said, without even turning around.

"Mary Belle?" Callie came to stand beside me. "I have an idea. How about if Amarius makes us —"

She saw the look on my face.

"No, wait!" she said. "Listen! Amarius wants to make us chicken tonight, and then tomorrow night we'll have the pea soup and *he* wants some of that. A trade — he asked for it."

"How come?"

"How come what? How come he wants pea soup?"

"Yeah, how come he wants pea soup?"

"Because he loves it. He said so. Pea soup with ham hocks, he said. It's Dearly's favorite, too, he said."

"Yeah, well there's no ham hocks in this soup. Just hot dogs."

"That's all right — they won't care."

I slid the account book back in the desk and went to the porch to talk to Amarius myself, but he wasn't there.

"Where'd he go?" I asked.

"Home, I guess. Maybe to fry the chicken."

"Will you stop with the fried chicken? You'd think you were starving!"

But then I looked at her — skinny little arms, big eyes sunken in her little face — and thought, Maybe she is hungry. Not starved, but hungry. So let her have some fried chicken. Let us all have some, me and Ariel, too. Do us all good.

Callie came and wrapped her arms around my waist. "You're having a hard time, aren't you?" she said.

I had heard — I knew they were Amarius's words. But still, they were so honest, so sincere coming out of her mouth that I didn't know whether to laugh or cry.

Callie was looking up at me, hugging me, laughter in her eyes. Like she knew she'd won.

I hugged her back and looked away.

"You are a mess!" I told her, choosing some of Amarius's words, just as she had. "A real mess."

"But you love me anyway," she said.

I do. Oh, Lord, yes I do.

I didn't say it though. I just untwined her arms from around my waist. "You win!" I said.

"I know," she said.

Chapter 9

Amarius came to dinner that night — came bringing dinner that night. Usually he walks everywhere, but this time he came in his ancient black pickup truck, bringing all this food. Ariel came home early from the gas station, and we all ate together. It was like a birthday party or maybe like Christmas or Thanksgiving. There was so much food — there's never been so much food at one meal, not even when Mama was still here.

Amarius brought not only the fried chicken, but string beans cooked with bacon and onions, and corn bread and mashed potatoes — smashed potatoes, Callie called them. The potatoes had big hunks of butter melting in them, and there was even dessert — chocolate ripple ice cream. Did Amarius know that chocolate ripple was my favorite?

"You really made this?" Callie asked. "Or did Dearly help you?"

It seemed funny to hear Callie call Miss Dearly plain Dearly. Even Amarius called her Miss Dearly. Callie was the only one Miss Aikens let call her by her first name.

"I cook better'n Miss Dearly any day," Amarius said with a chuckle.

When the fried chicken had been passed and everyone had been served potatoes and beans and all, we bowed our heads to say the prayer.

When there's just us, Ariel always prays, but this time he turned to Amarius. "Would you say the blessing?" Ariel asked.

Amarius nodded.

There was a long pause while he seemed to be thinking. After a while, he spoke. "Lord," he said, and his voice was soft, confidential, as though he were speaking to a long-time friend. "We're gathered here to take this food together. We need your company. The children need you, I need you. Bless this child."

He stretched out one big hand toward Callie on one side of him. "And this child," he said, stretching another hand toward Ariel on the other side.

He looked up at me at the end of the table. "And," he added, "that child I can't reach.

"Join us here. Help us all.

"Amen."

"Amen," we all said.

We began to eat.

For a while, we were quiet, just concentrating on all that food, but after a while everyone began to talk.

Ariel, always quiet when he's with Callie and me, talked a lot to Amarius. And Callie seemed happier and livelier than I'd seen her in ages, maybe since Mama left. Come to think of it, Callie always seemed happiest when Amarius or Ariel were around. Was it just that she liked men better? Or was it me who made her get all quiet and drawn up like that?

Maybe, I supposed, maybe if I could stop worrying and fussing, I'd probably be more fun to be with.

I listened to Amarius and Ariel, watched Callie bouncing around in her chair, interrupting and laughing. And eating. I hadn't seen her eat that much since Mama left.

I stayed quiet, watching, studying them all. Maybe if I could learn to listen the way Amarius was listening to Ariel, then Ariel would talk more to me? Maybe if I could tease and play with Callie the way Ariel does, then maybe I could make Callie be happier?

No one seemed to notice that I was quiet, and that was fine with me. I was not sulking, only studying, because Lord knows, I needed to learn about them. But after a while, I began to be lonesome, right there at the table with them all. They were laughing and planning and talking. Callie was exaggerating about how our garden would have the biggest tomatoes in the whole county and how all by herself she could win the prize at the county fair come summer. She sounded so sure she could do it that at that moment, even I — who knew how she overwatered and overloved everything in every garden — even I believed she could do it.

And Ariel, he was telling Amarius about the gas station and the men there and about what they talked about, especially how they talked about girls. He talked about cars and about the things he found under the hoods of cars when he went to check the oil. He said one day a man drove into the garage and said, "Please will you check under the hood? There is a screeching under there and a nasty smell." Ariel lifted the hood, and there, right on top of the engine, was half a cat. At least, it looked like half a cat. Ariel was sure it was dead, but when he reached in, the cap leapt up and streaked away into the woods behind the garage, and no one has seen it since. So it hadn't been half a cat but a full cat, hunkered down on the engine, its body on top, its head hanging down, hanging on for dear life.

Callie and Amarius said things like, "Oh! That poor cat!" And then when the cat jumped up and ran off, everyone laughed, even me.

After we had stuffed ourselves so full that we couldn't possibly eat another bite, I got up to clear the table.

Callie helped me, and Ariel and Amarius went out on the porch, just like men do, like they were the papa and grandpapa. Some days that would have made me mad, but to tell the truth, that night I was glad to have them outside out of my way.

Callie and I spooned ice cream into bowls, Callie

making a dish of ice cream for Miss Mannie, too, and we took the ice cream outside.

It was already almost dark on the porch. Cicadas and peepers were making a racket in the grass at the pond, and one or two fireflies had already arrived to flit about under the darkest trees.

The men were sitting on the steps. Men. Funny word for Ariel, but I guess he is a man now. I went to the swing where I often sat with Callie. She didn't come to sit beside me, though. She went down the steps and wedged herself between Ariel and Amarius, as confident as though she was Miss Mannie, so sure they'd want her there.

Ariel slid an arm around her but didn't look at her and went right on talking. I don't think I've heard him talk that much in my whole entire life.

The lonesome feeling just seemed to fill me up.

I swung my swing hard.

On and on, on and on Ariel went, about school, the garage, the cars.

So why didn't I come down to listen, to be with them? Why was I setting myself apart? It struck me then that I was acting as mean and spoiled as Ellie Mae. Ariel was allowed to talk to someone else besides me. Callie was allowed to laugh and talk with others besides me. I was acting like a spoiled brat, as Mama would have said.

The moon shone down on us now, making the floorboards silver in its light, and I could see that Amarius was watching me, seeming to frown slightly.

Did I forget to wash my hair again?

"Miz Ma'y Belle," he said. "It'll be better soon. You just have to be the mama now, I know. But it'll be better soon, you wait and see."

Lord, was it that obvious?

"Mary Belle has always had to be the mama," Ariel said softly. "Mama knew nothing about how to be a mama."

He knew! He'd known all along?

I swallowed hard but found that I could not speak.

"Even a mama's got to rest sometimes," Amarius said, still looking at me.

She does, oh, Lord, yes. I blinked hard against the tears, but they were not sad tears.

I got up from the swing and came down the steps. I sat on my favorite place on the wide railing. Miss Mannie came nosing her big red head into my lap, to see if I had ice cream left. I did, a little, and let her lick the rest of the dish.

Ariel had stopped talking, just sort of fell quiet. He'd say a sentence or two, and then he'd be quiet, then another word or two, and then be quiet for a longer time, as though he had run down at last.

Callie was breathing softly, her head against Ariel's arm. I couldn't see her face in the dark, but I thought from the sweet evenness of her breathing that she was probably sleeping.

Amarius sat tall and still, his legs thrust out before him, his back as straight as the rifle he had rested last night against the porch. Yet I could tell that although he sat so upright and tall, he was completely relaxed, quiet and still in his soul.

The crickets sang. The tree frogs chattered. The fireflies disappeared into the night. Above the trees, the moon rose suddenly, slipping higher and higher into the sky as though thrust there by a giant hand. And still we sat.

Lord, it was so peaceful.

I began to wonder: could I ever stop watching and guarding? Could I rest my head back as Callie did? What could hurt us? Nothing now. Amarius would guard our secret. We had a garden and food and a little more money, now that summer was coming on.

Let in the crickets, let in the tree frogs, let in the moon and the silence. Even the deer who guards must sleep sometimes.

I breathed deep and slow and leaned back against the railing.

Callie struggled up, sat up, and, still half asleep, she leaned over the step. Then, with a little choking sound, she threw up.

Chapter 10

I should have known to not let Callie eat so much. She hadn't eaten that much since Mama went away, and her stomach wasn't used to it. I should have told her so. Actually, I had thought of it once at supper and was going to say, "Slow down, Callie. You'll be sick." But I hadn't, and now I wished I had.

I took her inside and bathed her and dried her and helped her into her nightgown. She was pale still when I tucked her into bed, but she was strong. She put her arms around my neck when she lay down, hugging me so tight I almost choked.

"'Night," she said. "Thank you."

"For what?"

"Supper."

"I didn't make it."

"I know."

"Silly," I said. I unwound her arms from around my neck and laid her back gently on her pillow. "Go to sleep now," I said. "You feel okay?"

"I'm okay."

"'Night, then," I said.

"'Night," she answered.

I was almost out of the room when she said, "Mary Belle?"

"Hmm?"

"I love you," she said.

"I know," I said. "Go to sleep now."

She sighed softly, as if she were almost, already, falling into sleep. "You and Miss Mannie," she said dreamily.

Me and Miss Mannie?

"What about Ariel?" I asked, laughing.

She didn't answer, and from her breathing, I could tell that she was already sleeping.

So why couldn't I say the words? Why could I not say, "I love you too, Callie"? I do, so how come I can't say it? Is it because if I say it, say those words, she will go away, too?

Out on the porch, Amarius and Ariel were still sitting there, the steps shining wet between them where Ariel had hosed away the throw-up.

They were talking again, although it was Amarius this time who was talking. He stopped when I came onto the porch.

I took my place again on the railing.

"Callie better?" Ariel said.

"She's okay. I shouldn't have let her eat so much."

"My fault," Amarius said. "Too much fried chicken."

How could it be your fault? I thought. You didn't make her eat it. But I didn't say that because I knew how it was to feel responsible.

We continued to sit there quietly for a while, but it seemed to me that any peace that had been around us before was gone. There was something like tension or maybe worry between Amarius and Ariel, almost as though they had been arguing or talking about something worrisome. Could it be? Why? And about what?

I sat on there for a while, hoping they'd talk again, that Ariel would speak, hoping to feel that smooth, soothing sound of his voice going on and on the way it did before. Even though it had made me feel sad and left out before, I wanted it now, wanted to know that he was happy enough to want to talk. I wanted, too, for Amarius to say something like he said before, that he knew — maybe — what it was like to be me.

But even though I sat for a long while, they didn't start talking again, and there was no calm out there in the quiet. So after a while, I got up off the steps and went back inside to wash up the dishes.

There was a lot of work to do. Company makes more dishes. I guess I hadn't known that before since we hardly ever had company. There were also loads of leftovers that I didn't know what to do with. Should I wrap them up and give them back to Amarius? We could sure use the food, but it was really his and Miss Dearly's. But if I gave it back, would it hurt his feelings?

So what I decided to do was keep some and give some back. I divided it in half, half for us, half for him. But even in half, there was an awful lot of food. Amarius must have done three whole chickens for just the four of us.

When I crossed to the door to take out the garbage, I could hear Amarius and Ariel talking. I heard Callie's name. But as soon as I stepped out on the porch, they stopped talking again.

I dropped the garbage bag on the porch behind Ariel. "Put this in the can," I said. Because I felt angry and left out again, the words came out meaner than I meant them to. "Please," I added. "And don't forget to put the stone back on top."

That was so the raccoons wouldn't get into the trash cans at night, although sometimes, even with the stone on top, they got in. We'd see them standing on the cans and rocking them back and forth till the cans tipped over and spilled on the ground.

Ariel nodded. "I'll do it," he said. "You can leave the rest of the dishes if you want. I'll do them when I come in."

"It's okay," I said. I kept standing there.

Ariel kept on looking at me. "Don't worry," he said. "I'll put the stone on top."

"I know."

I still stood there.

Neither of them spoke again. So I went back inside, slamming the screen door and then, to make sure that they knew that I knew that they were closing me out, I slammed the inside door, too. There! Let them talk without me listening. I didn't care.

I washed and wiped the dishes, then put them back in the cupboard. Then I swept the floor and wiped down the tabletop and stove.

Dummies! Both of them. What was I supposed to be — too young to hear what the "grown-ups" were talking about? Since when was Ariel the only grown-up around? What about me? If I was such a kid, let Ariel do the dishes, the washing, the taking care of Callie.

Or was it because he now thought he was a man, he and Amarius together, men who couldn't talk around the women? Was it because he was such a big deal at the garage, talking about "the girls"?

Stupid men!

I went in my room to check on Callie.

Her bed is across the room from mine, and the moon was bright and lit the room with a soft, silver glow. I stood beside the bed and watched her sleep. She was peaceful, her chest moving softly, lips parted a little. Sleeping like that, her arm wrapped tight around her rag dog, she looked younger than in the day. She was all right now. She had just eaten too much.

She had no covers over her, and her nightdress had climbed up. I bent and smoothed it over her, so she would not be so naked in the moonlight.

She was hot where I touched her, her skin as hot as though she had been out in the noon sun.

I put the back of my hand gently against her forehead, the way I had seen Mama do.

Callie sighed, and her breathing changed rhythm — became quick and short, as though she were dreaming of running. But when I took my hand away, she settled back into a soft kind of breathing.

She had a fever.

Well, she'd be better in the morning. And maybe she'd learn not to stuff herself next time.

What should I do next? I was too wide awake to sleep, and I couldn't turn on a light in there to read. I could read in the kitchen or the bathroom, but I didn't feel like doing that. What I wanted to do was sit on the porch in the moonlight the way I had been doing lately. Except that Ariel and Amarius were there, and they'd stop talking, would shut me out if I came out.

I stood at the window, looking out at the yard in the moonlight.

Bats flew from the hollow tree back by the fence, flitting across the face of the moon. Graceful in flight, like swallows, swallows-of-the-night. Why were people scared of bats, I wondered. Tiny furry creatures, when you saw them up close, wings closed, small creatures with wings to make them soar, not tied to the earth the way people are.

I pictured my heart as a bat — wings folded, furry small animal inside my chest.

A hateful heart.

Because if Mama came back, I would trip her up and break her ankle so she'd never dance again.

I went to the front door and looked through the glass.

Amarius was standing and Ariel was, too, one on either side of the bottom step. They seemed to be talking, although I couldn't hear what they said. They leaned toward each other, heads close, as though they were parentheses, curving one toward the other.

Quietly, I eased open the inside door. I needed air, it was stuffy in here. But yes, it's true that I was spying.

The inside door was quiet on its hinges; only the screen door screeched.

Slowly, I opened the inside door.

The breeze blew in, and with it, their voices. One after the other, like in singing class at school, point, counterpoint.

They were saying good night, and saying a good-night prayer.

I heard them pray. "Our Father," they said.

"Who art in heaven . . .

"Thy will be done . . .

"Give us this day our daily bread . . ."

And I? Oh, how I wished I could say those things and mean them. I believed there was a moon and that bats flew at dusk. I believed that mamas and papas ran away and little sisters ate too much and got sick sometimes. I believed that big sisters have to be in charge, to be on guard.

I did not believe that someone did this for me, that someone would give us our bread. Ariel had to go out and make the money, and I had to go out and get and cook the food for us. I did not believe what they believed. But I did wish it were true.

Chapter 11

Next day was Saturday and no school, and Callie stayed in bed all day. She said she felt better, but she looked tired, so I made her stay there, and Sunday, too.

Ariel went to church and then to work. I had work to do, too. The May Fair parade would be that Friday, the last day of school, and I still had to finish Callie's dress. I had cut the bottom off Mama's dress and had taken in the side seams till it hugged Callie's waist just right. Then I had covered my stitches with a wide pink ribbon from a dress Callie had outgrown years ago. It looked good, and no one would guess it was an old dress of Mama's. All I had to do was hem it up now.

It was late morning, and the sun was shining hot when I took the dress into our room for Callie to try on.

Callie was awake, sitting up in bed reading, the covers up to her chin.

"Aren't you hot?" I said. I held out the dress. "Try this on? I want to hem it."

She pushed back the covers, threw her legs over the side of the bed and stood up.

"I can't wait," she said. "I get to throw the candies and everything."

"Did you pick your Queen's Court yet?" I asked.

I had finally persuaded her not to have me in the court, but she hadn't told me who else in class she had chosen.

"Naomi Lynn," she said, "and that's all!" Her face clouded up.

"That's all? Don't you have to pick others?"

"I'm supposed to but I won't. I told Miss Callahan she could do it. Everybody gets mad if they're not picked. So I picked just Naomi Lynn, and Miss Callahan can pick the rest."

Callie stripped off her nightgown and stood before me wearing only her underwear.

Lord, her ribs stuck out!

I slid the dress over her head.

"Gos m' squinch," she said, her head inside the dress.

"What?"

She pulled the dress down over her. "Got to switch, or I tried to. I wanted to switch the parade from last of the day to the beginning part."

"Why?"

"So I can play! The May Queen has to wear her white dress all day. I told Miss Callahan I can't stand around like a statue of me all day, just to keep my dress clean for the parade."

"What'd she say?"

I pulled the dress smooth over Callie, then knelt down in front of her with the box of pins.

But something was wrong here.

"She said no," Callie said, "but she said I could wear play clothes all day and then change after." Callie paused. "But you know what else she said?"

Something was wrong with this dress.

"Hold still, Callie," I said.

"I am!"

"Well, why doesn't this fit?"

"'Cause you didn't finish it yet, silly."

"That's not what I mean. It doesn't fit here!"

I took a handful of dress at her waist and pinched it between my fingers. It was big for her, way too big for her. But I took it in to fit just two, three weeks ago. It fit her then.

"Callie!" I said. "Hold still."

"I am still!"

"Well, why doesn't this fit anymore?"

"How do I know?"

"Did you lose more weight?" I said. And my voice was much more scared than I wanted it to be.

I looked up at her. Her face was very pink, as if I had caught her doing something she wasn't supposed to be doing.

She shrugged. "I ate a lot last night."

She had. And she got sick, too.

She *was* sick! Was she sick? Little kids are supposed to grow, not get littler. I'd have to take her to the doctor. But then he'd know! He was the one who'd called the county people last time, the time I got cut and they took Callie and me away. Oh, Lord, yes they did. She was getting plain skinny, right in front of me she was sliding away, and I knew suddenly, or I thought I knew, what Ariel and Amarius had been talking about last night. Callie. They were worried, too.

I could feel my throat tighten as if someone had put a giant cord around it. And I felt — Lord, I felt like I wanted to cry.

I bent my head and began pinning up the dress.

I pinned it front, back, sides, turning Callie this way, round a little more, no more, okay, now back this way, till the dress was pinned, and till I wasn't feeling like crying anymore.

"Okay now," I said. "Arms up."

I helped her take the dress off. Then quickly, I slid the nightgown back over her head. Covered her skinniness, quick, before I saw again what I did not want to know.

But I did see something like a rash, some redness on her stomach, and a few blisters on the tops of her thighs.

"What's this, Callie?" I asked. "This rash, how long have you had this?"

"I don't know."

"Does it hurt?"

"No."

"Itch?"

"Some."

"What do you mean, some?"

"Stop picking at me! I'm all right!"

She tugged down her nightie, then jumped into bed and pulled the sheet up to her chin, glaring at me. "Now leave me alone! You stare at me like I'm weird or something."

"Not weird," I said.

I smiled at her. Oddly, I felt relieved. She probably just had the chicken pox or measles or maybe German measles. Everybody at school had had something lately.

"You probably have chicken pox," I said.

"No!" She burst out crying. "I won't be able to be May Queen!"

"Yes, you will. You started being sick Friday night. Then Saturday." I counted on my fingers — four days, five days. "By Wednesday or Thursday you'll be fine," I said.

"What if I'm not?" Tears were streaming down her face.

"You will be."

"Promise?"

I was tempted to promise. But how could I do that? "I can't promise," I said. "But I know you will be."

"Miss Callahan wants to see Mama at the May Fair."

"What!?? Why? Are you in trouble?"

The cord tightened around my neck again. Oh, Lord, what had Callie done now?

"No, I'm not in trouble. Miss Callahan just said she

bet Mama was so proud of me for being May Queen and she couldn't wait till the May Fair to talk to Mama and tell her how proud of me she was, too, and that's all, so there!"

"What'd you say then?"

Callie took a deep breath. "Nothing. I said nothing."

"Really? Promise? Look at me, Callie, do you promise?"

"Why should I promise when you won't?"

"Callie, you are *so* irritating! I can't promise, because I don't know if you'll be better. But you know what you said."

"Well, I didn't say anything, so there."

"Okay. Okay."

But then, was it worse that she didn't say anything? Would Miss Callahan suspect something wrong? Is that why she'd said she wanted to see Mama?

But I could not worry about that now. I could not. The May Fair was the last day of school, and if Mama wasn't there, well, so what? After that, there was no school so no one would come poking at us. And maybe by fall Mama would be back, although I didn't really think so.

I was almost out of the room when Callie yelled, "I want Mama back!"

"Callie." I turned to her. "You know —"

"I know!" She glared at me. "I know, she's gone and she's not coming back, that's what you say. But she is. I know it. And I can still want her even if you say she's not coming back. I do still want her!"

What could I say? Of course she wanted Mama. She was only seven years old. Besides, she and Mama danced together. I only watched. And even I was wanting Mama back.

"And you don't even care!" Callie said. "You're glad she's gone, so you can be the boss."

That was so mean! That was so, so mean!

But Callie's eyes were filled up with tears, and I recognized that the pink in her face was not because she was embarrassed. She burned with fever, I could see that now. I remembered measles, remembered telling Mama that I wanted Papa back because Papa would be nicer to me. I remembered how I felt.

"I want Mama!" Callie wailed again, and she banged her fist against the bed.

I remembered how I'd felt, how she must have been feeling, but the remembering didn't do me any good. If I had remembered better and it had done me any good, I would have done what Mama did — sit beside her on the bed, wipe her forehead and say, "I know, I know how bad you feel."

But I didn't. I didn't say the mean things that I thought because I know how words can haunt you. But I was mad. She had no right to be so mean. Instead, I just left her there and went outside and slammed her door.

I suppose I should have known that things like slamming doors, that things like that can haunt you, too.

Chapter 12

The next week was hard — all of the next week was hard, because Callie was sick. Really, really sick. By Sunday night she was covered with big red spots, and she cried and went half crazy with the itching.

I tried everything I could think of to make her better, and when Ariel came home from work, he tried, too. We both remembered that there is not too much you can do for measles but wait for it to be over and to take cornstarch baths for itching. And aspirin, we decided, aspirin to make her fever come down and because she said she had a headache.

Mama had cornstarch in the cabinet over the stove, so we made up baths for Callie and we took turns reading to her and sitting by her bed. I was not so worried about her as I had been before. Measles, I knew, you got better from quick. It was just that it felt so bad at first. But it would be over after a few days or a week or so and then you were allowed to go out, even if you were pretty spotty looking for a while.

So we took turns, Ariel and me, staying home from school. I stayed home Monday, and Ariel stayed home Tuesday, and then Wednesday I stayed home again.

On Tuesday at school, everybody was asking about Callie.

"Is she still sick?" Anna Tilley asked.

I shrugged. "Just a little. It's just measles."

"She's too sick to be May Queen, I bet," Ellie Mae chimed in.

"No! She's not too sick for that. She'll be better in another day," I said. And then I added, "Mama said so."

"I'll ask Miss Callahan if I can do it," Ellie Mae said. "I know how since I did it already. I still have my May Queen dress from last year."

Anna Tilley and I exchanged looks, and Anna Tilley looked as if she'd burst out laughing.

I knew exactly what she was thinking, same thing I was: Fat old Ellie Mae, bet anything her dress wouldn't fit from last year.

And anyway, Callie *was* going to be better soon.

She was, too. Wednesday when I stayed home with her was a good day. Callie had pretty much stopped itching and was sleeping most of the day, so I didn't have to play Go Fish or checkers or read to her all of the time.

Each day Amarius came by and looked in on us.

On Wednesday, he stood for a long time by Callie's bed where she was sleeping. He was there so long that

I tiptoed out of the room. I thought that he was praying.

He came out to the porch, where I sat hemming the white dress. There was still a chance that Callie could be May Queen. If she was much better tonight, and if she didn't come out with any new spots, then she could rest tomorrow, and on Friday, the last day of school, the day of the May Fair, she could go and be queen.

"She's resting," Amarius said. He closed the screen door softly behind him and stood there, his hand still on the handle.

"She's better," I said.

Amarius was quiet for a while. "Maybe we should get a doctor," he said finally.

"A doctor? Why? He'd want to know about Mama. Callie's better — you can see that."

"Maybe, maybe not." He went down the steps. "I'll be back later," he said.

"Amarius! Don't you call anyone!" I called after him.

"I won't, not just yet," he said. He disappeared in the direction of the garden.

So why was he worried? I wasn't worried now that Callie was better.

Very carefully, I finished the hem of the dress. If Callie slept all day, she'd be better — I knew it. That night we would try on the dress and it would fit and where it was still a little loose, we'd pull it tight with the pink sash. Callie would still have marks, but she'd be all right. She hadn't popped out with new spots since last night.

I held up the dress. A pretty dress now. No one would

ever guess that it once was a mama's dancing dress. It was perfect for a girl now, for Callie, a pretty May Day dress.

I took it to our room.

Callie was still sleeping, and I hung the dress on a hanger from the closet door so she would see it when she woke up. She'd be happy to see it finished.

I went and stood beside the bed.

Callie looked peaceful and quiet, her breath slow and sweet, in and out, in and out, between her slightly parted lips.

I wished she'd wake up. I was needing someone to talk to.

I put a hand on her forehead, testing her temperature. Hoping she'd wake up.

She did. Her eyes flew open and she looked at me, but it was a blank kind of look, as though she were sleeping with her eyes wide open.

"Hi," I said. "How do you feel?"

"Mary Belle?" she said.

"No!" I laughed. "Did you think I was Ariel?"

She frowned and looked around the room. "Did we get a new rug?" she asked.

"A what?"

"A new rug?" she said again.

"What rug?"

She sat up in bed.

"This. Here." She looked at the floor. "Is it new?"

There was no rug on our bedroom floor, no rug at all.

"Callie, stop being a jerk."

"Mama bought it, I bet," she said. She lay back down.

"Bought what?"

"The rug."

I was going to cry, oh, Lord, I would cry. Not this, not this.

Callie's eyes closed, and in a minute, she was breathing deeply, sound asleep.

I stood watching her sleep. So that was all! She was still deep in a dream when she'd sat up and was talking in her sleep. When she woke up next time she would be better, and I would tell her what she had said and we would laugh together.

I went to the kitchen and made us both some lunch. Peanut butter sandwich for me and soup from a can for Callie.

Callie had eaten the pea soup I had made on Sunday, but right after, she threw it up. She threw up everything she'd eaten since Saturday, except for canned chicken broth.

So I opened another can of chicken broth and put it in a pan on the stove. I left it on low, ready for Callie when she woke up. I took my sandwich to the porch and ate it standing up, looking out over the fields. No deer here in the middle of the day. Nothing moving in the shimmering sun.

Restless. I could not sit.

I went back in the house, wandered from room to room. I found myself in Mama's room. I usually stayed away from there, except for the time I went to raid her closet for Callie's dress. But for some reason that day, I needed to be there. I fingered things — the few dresses she'd left, her blankets on the bed, the curtains at the window. Her powder box in the drawer of her dresser that smelled like old people.

I opened the old jewelry box on her dresser. It had a music box inside that once played "Silent Night," but it hadn't worked in years. I wondered if I could take it apart and fix it. "Silent Night" is such a pretty, simple song. The box was stuffed with broken beads and single earrings. Nothing worth anything. There were pictures on her dresser in silver frames, one picture of Callie, one of Ariel, one of me. Each of us at one year old, taken sitting on a puffy blanket on a table. I bet someone had paid a photographer good money to take those pictures, but for some reason, I didn't think Mama would have done that. Papa maybe? Papa would have done that.

Maybe we should sell the silver frames to get some money, I thought. Maybe we could even sell her furniture, her bed.

But she would be awful mad to have no place to sleep if ever she did come home.

Maybe I could use her bed, use her room even. That way, I wouldn't have to share a room with Callie. It was a pain sharing a room, like last night when I couldn't even turn on a light to read.

I sat down on the bed, then lay back, testing it. I stretched myself out. The mattress felt good, better than my mattress.

But no, I thought, get up quick. Lying in that bed felt spooky, scary even.

I went back to the porch.

I was so restless. Something was coming, something I could not sit still for, something I did not want to wait for. It was coming, and it could not catch me sitting down.

I knew what to do. I could walk out the lane to the road for the mail.

I put on shoes because there are bees and things that when you step on them they don't feel good. It's a long walk to the mailbox, and some days we forget the mail entirely and it's there for two or three days before we remember, especially Friday till Monday. On most school days, I walk past the mailbox, so those days I don't forget. But it doesn't matter because we don't get mail that matters usually, only bills and ads.

It looked the same that day. The electric bill. A grocery store ad. An ad that said, Unscramble these letters, and you can win a fur coat. And a letter from Mama.

A letter from Mama! It was from Mama. I knew her handwriting, her purple pen — she had even taken her purple ballpoint pen with her. It was not addressed to me, not to Callie. Only to Ariel. It even said on it: "Private," it said. Underlined. Private.

Lord. What did she want? She was coming home. She wanted to know how we were. She was sending money.

I could open the letter. It wouldn't matter that it was private, would it? She was mother to us all, not just to Ariel.

I stood by the box for a long time, the letter shaking in my hand.

Open it! It is from your mama.

But Ariel, when he came home, he would be mad.

So what did that matter?

Oh, yes, maybe she was coming home, and I could tell Callie, "She's coming home, Callie, she's coming home. You can get better, and Mama will be home."

I looked around, the letter in my hand.

No one was watching. No one was anywhere at all around. Only a blackbird sat in a pine tree way off to my right, way up at the top, the branch waving slightly with his weight.

I turned back toward the house.

Chapter 13

I went all the way back to the house before I opened that letter. I went up the porch steps and sat on the swing and opened it. I did not steam it open the way I had thought of doing. I just plain opened it. But my hand was shaking so that I tore the envelope and it ripped almost completely across. There would be no way now that Ariel would not know that the letter had been opened. But for now, I did not care at all about that.

I had to read the letter two times before I really understood it, and then I read it again, although what it said was plain enough. It was just hard to understand that anyone could write a letter like that, even her.

This is what it said:

Dear Ariel:

How are you? I am pretty good except for money. It costs a lot to live here, and what I get from my checks don't cover expenses. And something exciting, I'm dancing on the stage now! But I need money to buy some dancing dresses. Send me $50.00 as soon as you get this letter — you remember, I left $50.00 in the sugar bowl. If you used that all up already, take the money from your pay at the gas station. Send it to me, care of J. Brown, P.O. Box 791, Asheville, N.C.

I hope you are making out all right, you and the girls.

Much love,
Mama

P. S. The address is a box number of a friend who will send the money on to me. I am not in Asheville.

After I read the letter all those times, I read it again, trying to read between the lines. But there was nothing between the lines, just a letter telling us to send her money. But still I felt confused, as if there was something there that I should understand, but that I couldn't.

How are you?

We are not so good, Mama.

It costs a lot to live here.

Where?

I am dancing on the stage now.

But Callie needs you.

I hope you are making out all right.

We were. But we are not so good now. Callie is not so good.

I sat on that swing for a long time, thinking — thinking about this letter and that last letter. The last letter, her good-bye letter, it had said sweet things — you mean everything in the world to me, take care of yourselves and Callie, do. And then this one, it just said, send money, do not try to find me, I am dancing on the stage. But those two letters were the same really, the meaning was the same: I am gone away. I do not want to be with you anymore.

Sitting there in that swing, I made up letters to answer her, pretending at first that I was Ariel, because of course, she should not know that it was me who opened her letter:

Dear Mama:

Where are you? I'll send money when you tell me where you are.

Much love,
Ariel

Or:

Dear Mama:
No.
Much love,
Ariel

Or else:

Dear Mama:

Please come home. Callie is sick and she needs you. There is no money left, and if we send you this week's pay, there will not be enough money left for food.

From your daughter,
Mary Belle

P.S. You said Callie needed special care, but I haven't given her special care and she's very sick. I'm sorry. I have been trying.

Sitting there with the letter in my hand, the shaking began, and it took a long time for it to stop. All over I shook. It made me dizzy and weak, as though I were falling down a well, falling, falling, and I wondered if that's what Mama felt, when she said she felt as if she were fading.

Suddenly I thought — the postmark! The postmark would tell me.

I smoothed the envelope, but there was no postmark, not even a stamp. She — or someone — had put the letter in our mailbox! Did that mean she was nearby? Even now she might be near, lurking, watching me, watching me read her letter to Ariel.

I stood up. "Mama?" I called softly. "Mama?"

I listened. Nothing.

"Mama? Callie's sick, you know."

Only the locusts answered me.

I went to the edge of the porch. My hands were shaking again. I leaned over the railing, looking toward the back of the house.

No one. Nobody at all.

I knew what she'd done. She had sent the letter to a friend in town who'd put it our mailbox. But who would do that? Who else but us knew that Mama was gone? Mama didn't have many friends.

I felt spooky suddenly, exposed, as if eyes were watching me, eyes I couldn't see.

I took the letter into the house to find a hiding place for it. I wouldn't tell Ariel. He'd send the money, and we couldn't afford that. I didn't think it right to send her Ariel's hard-earned money.

I went into my room. Stupid me — the only hiding place I could think of was under my mattress. Not very good, but that's all I could think of.

I looked at Callie in her bed. Her eyes were still closed, and she was sound asleep. I slid the letter under my mattress and then went across the room and sat on the side of her bed.

"Callie?" I said softly.

Dumb to sleep all day. She'd be awake all night now.

"Callie?"

She didn't stir.

"Callie, do you want something to eat? Some soup?"

I shook her slightly.

She opened her eyes, but didn't seem to see me sitting there.

"Callie? You awake?"

She didn't answer.

"Callie, wake up. You still dreaming?"

She nodded.

"Well, wake up. Want some soup?"

"Okay," she said. Her voice was cracked sounding, froggy and hoarse.

"I'll go get it. How do you feel?"

"Headache." She moved her hand slightly toward her head, but then let the hand fall back on the sheet.

"I'll get you some aspirin, okay? I'll be right back with it."

She nodded and sighed.

"Need to go to the bathroom first?" I asked.

She nodded, a small nod.

"Well, sit up. I'll help you get up."

She tried to sit up, but immediately lay back down again, as though moving were just too much work.

"Come on," I said. "You haven't been out of bed all day."

I boosted her up to a sitting position, then held her as she put her feet on the floor. But she just closed her eyes and lay back against my arm, all her weight against me.

Okay, she didn't have to go.

"All right," I said. "Lie down then. You can go later after you eat, okay?"

She didn't answer or even move. She just lay back against the pillow, her eyes closed, her legs still hanging over the edge of the bed, her feet against the floor.

I lifted her legs, swung them into the bed, then covered her up.

I won't think, oh, Lord, I won't think that she's very sick.

I went out to the kitchen, reheated the soup, poured

it in a bowl, got some aspirin and water and a glass, and put it all on a tray. Then I carried the tray back into our room.

Callie was awake now, her eyes wide. "Where's Mama?" she asked.

"Mama? Callie, I —"

"I love her dancing dress," Callie whispered. "Did she show you how it spins out?"

"Where? When?"

Oh, Lord, had she really come back?

Callie looked past me, over my shoulder, smiling. "Mama?" she whispered. She held her arms out wide for just a moment. "Oh, Mama!" she whispered. "Mama, let's dance!"

I whirled around, feeling goose bumps prickling on my arms.

No Mama. Of course not.

I turned back to Callie. "Callie, don't be — Callie, have some soup. It'll make you feel better. You'll wake up better."

"She went in the bathroom, I bet," Callie whispered, and she looked exhausted just from holding her arms out for that minute. "I'll go get her."

She moved as though she'd try and get out of bed.

"I'll look," I said. "Stay there."

I put the tray on the dresser and went in the bathroom. Of course Mama wasn't there. Callie was dreaming still, a fever dream, Mama would have said.

I went back to our room. "She's not there," I said.

"Who?" Callie said.

"Mama! Remember? You said . . . Never mind. Sit up and eat this."

I picked up the bowl and spoon and sat on the bed. I put an arm around Callie's shoulder and half lifted her.

Her head rested against my shoulder. Funny, she was so thin, yet her head was heavy.

"Take a little," I said, holding the spoon up to her mouth.

I opened my own mouth as if doing that would get her to open hers.

But she didn't. She just breathed deeply as though she were falling asleep again.

"Callie?"

No answer.

"Callie!"

I looked down at her. She was sound asleep on my shoulder, her breathing fast and shallow as if she had been running.

Amarius was right. We needed a doctor. She needed a doctor.

Oh, Lord, I did not want to cope with this, I did not want to deal with this. Callie was sick, really sick. And Lord — oh, Mama! — I did not know what to do.

Chapter 14

I did not know what to do, but I knew I could not do nothing. Something bad had happened to Callie since early that morning. Her regular girl self was gone, leaving this spirit child that talked nonsense and saw things that weren't there.

Callie couldn't go far away. I had to help her, to bring her back.

I ran all the way to Amarius's house, a mile just about, in the hot sun. I must have been a sight, too, because Miss Dearly Aikens, when she opened the door, she just stared at me for a second.

"Mary Belle!" she said. "What's wrong?"

"Callie's sick. We need a doctor. Can Amarius come? Come now? Can I use your phone?"

We have a phone at home. I could have called from

there. I could have saved all this time running here, but my brain was not working good that day.

"Come in, come in!" she said. "Please do."

I stood there rooted to the porch. "It's really important."

"I know. I'll be fast, But come in out of the sun while I get my car keys."

Car keys? But I need Amarius. I need a doctor.

She was holding the door wide, so I came in.

I had never been in Amarius's house before, although I had walked past many times on the road. It was dark and cool inside, and it took my eyes a while to adjust.

The phone was on a desk in the far corner, under a low, long window. The floorboards were wide and polished, and a thin, bright rug lay in the center in a square of sunlight that I crossed to get to the desk.

And oh, there was the piano in the corner! A big one, too. I had never touched the keys of a piano, but I always dreamed that I could play one right away, if I ever sat down and tried. All of that music in my head, in my notebook, all of that music would come out through my fingers if I ever sat down at the piano.

A doctor. We need a doctor.

"May I use this phone?" I said, when Miss Dearly came out of the back room, her car keys in hand, an orange scarf tied like a turban around her hair. Oh, Callie, I thought, wait till you see — you'll love this scarf.

"Do you know the number?" she asked.

I didn't. I stood there feeling foolish.

"What doctor?" she asked, and her hand was already spinning the pages of the phone book to the yellow pages. She opened it to *Physicians*. I saw the heading.

How smart! I would have wasted a lot of time looking under "Doctors."

"Dr. Brody," I said.

She found his number and read it out to me.

I dialed and heard the connection click, and then the phone rang and a voice said, "Hello!"

I started to speak. "Callie's sick. Can the doctor come?"

"I'm sorry," the nurse or whoever said. "He's at the hospital seeing patients. He'll be back about two. Can I —"

I hung up.

"What?" Miss Dearly said.

"He's not there. He's at the hospital."

"But you hung up. You didn't leave a message?"

"No."

"I'll leave a message," Miss Dearly said gently.

She took the phone, dialed, and I heard her talking, asking for the doctor to call, to come to our house.

She left our name and phone number, and then we were out the door into the blinding sunlight and into the car and were speeding down the dirt road to the main road and across to home. We had to go the long way round, because a car cannot cut through a field, even if Callie is very sick.

We had to go slowly when we came to the rutted hill

to the house. I was grateful that Miss Dearly didn't speak or ask questions. We aren't great friends because we don't see each other much, but I like what I see. Practically everyone knows who she is and likes her — except for the big farm owners, they don't like her much. She works for the county government, and it's her job to be sure the workers on the farms have water and toilets in the fields and that their babies get their shots. She works, too, with all the civil rights people who come down from the North, but she doesn't seem to like them much. You see her everywhere, often with a baby in her arms. She doesn't have any babies of her own, so maybe that's why she likes to hold other people's babies.

When we finally got up the road to the house, she parked the car and we jumped out. I ran up the steps, and she followed behind, quick as can be.

I showed her the way to my room.

Callie looked much the same as before — quiet, sleeping, two bright red spots of color high on her cheeks. She was breathing fast though, as though she were running in her dreams.

Miss Dearly knelt beside the bed and took Callie's hand.

"Callie?" she said softly. "Callie?"

Callie did not open her eyes.

Miss Dearly bent close to Callie's face, did something with Callie's eyelids, pressed her fingers to Callie's wrist, then stood up.

"How long has she been like this?" she asked.

"Like this?"

"Unconscious," she said.

"She was talking to me just before I came to you," I said. "But I was scared because she wasn't making any sense. That's why —"

"I see. Do you have a thermometer in the house?"

We did. I brought it.

She didn't put it in Callie's mouth but slipped it under Callie's armpit. Then she sat on the bed, staring into Callie's face, one hand smoothing Callie's hair from her forehead.

Oh, don't look like that, so scared. She'll be all right.

Will she?

After a minute, Miss Dearly stood up, looked once at the thermometer, then at me.

"Your mama?" she said.

The moment I had been dreading. The very one.

I shrugged.

"Not here?" she said. "Amarius says —"

"Yes. She's gone."

"Ariel?"

"At school."

"We can't wait. She needs more than a doctor. A hospital, I think."

Oh, no, don't take her away!

"It's serious, Mary Belle. You know that. That's why you came to me."

"I didn't come for you. I came for Amarius."

"Amarius would tell you the same thing," she said.

"You won't let them keep her?" I said.

"Keep her?"

"You know. For good. Like to a foster home or something."

She frowned, and I could tell she wasn't understanding me. But how could she? Maybe she didn't know what had happened last time.

But all she said was, "Over my dead body."

And then the phone was ringing, and I ran to answer it. Dr. Brody! Now we wouldn't have to go to the hospital after all.

But it was not Dr. Brody. It was a voice I hadn't heard before, one I didn't know. It was an oily voice, a sneaky one. It asked for, "Your mother."

My mother. My mama wasn't there. For the second time that day I had to tell someone that. But this one, this one I wouldn't tell. This one didn't need to know.

"She's resting," I said.

"Resting? This is the Office of Education calling. Tell her it's important."

"I can't. I told you she's resting."

"It's two in the afternoon," the voice said.

Yes. It was. And the doctor would be back at two, and he would call.

"Then I can't talk to you any more," I said. "I'm expecting an important call."

I hung up the phone, feeling good and satisfied.

Miss Dearly was beside me. "You've done so well

taking care of things," she said, "but I think I'd better call the ambulance."

So she called and said to bring an ambulance, we have an emergency here, and ice packs, bring those, too.

They did. In a little while they were there, and they brought ice packs and an ambulance, and three big men carried Callie into the ambulance on a stretcher, but really, just one of them could have picked her up in their arms, she was so light, and they took her away.

Miss Dearly and I, we followed along behind.

Chapter 15

I heard the words, but I didn't believe what they were saying to me. The word I heard most was "grave."

Callie was in Isolation. Her condition was grave.

Grave like a grave in the ground?

"How can she joke at a time like this?" the one in the green doctor suit asked the other one.

Really, I wasn't joking. I just didn't know.

But more, I didn't believe what they were telling me. For two days they had been saying that Callie might not live, that is what "grave" means. And if she were to live, they say, her brain might not be right. Complications, they said, complications of measles.

Complications?

It was serious, it was critical, it was grave. She might have had a better chance if she had not been so run-down to begin with. She was terribly thin, weakened, not eating right at all, probably. Had she been worrying about something? Was something wrong at home?

Oh, didn't I take good care of her?

Then they moved her to Intensive Care.

Callie might be dying?

Yes.

But only maybe?

They looked at each other.

That was when I decided to close them out. I could close my mind, even my ears. I would sit here till Callie got better, and I wouldn't hear what they said.

I wouldn't leave the hospital waiting room, either. I had slept on the lumpy couch for two days, and I decided I wouldn't leave till Callie left with me. The first night, Ariel came and slept in that room, too. He skipped school that morning but then had to leave for work. Part of that first and second day, Miss Dearly was there, too. And always Amarius was there. He never left me. I hated to close him out, too, but I had to. You can't let in some things and keep others out. So this is what I did: I sat there and didn't hear one single thing that anyone said to me. I realized now how Ariel felt. Before this, I always needed things said, needed to hear the words. And Ariel was the one who didn't want to say them or hear them. But that was before, before when I didn't know about being really scared, when I only worried about things like money or food or Mama being gone. That was before Callie was in Intensive Care, before Callie was grave.

But when they came in all together, then it was harder not to hear them. I think it was the third day I had been there, when they came to me together, trying to make me listen to them, asking me questions. Their faces were kind looking, but fakey. I've seen that look before, on the faces of the ladies at foster care. There were four of them, two men, two women. One of the women wore a white doctor suit, and the man doctor was in a green doctor suit. The other man and lady were in regular suit suits, gray and dull. I wouldn't even look at them. I kept on reading my magazine, and after a while, when they wouldn't go away, I began to hum. I put the magazine down open in my lap, put my fingers in my ears, and hummed. If you hum good, with your fingers in your ears like that, you don't hear those words that they are saying at you.

I was humming and reading like that, when suddenly Amarius jumped up from the couch beside me. He jumped up so quick, that you could believe that he was young, instead of an old, old man.

He stuck his face up close to one of them, and I saw the green suit back up fast. Amarius who never fights with anyone.

They began moving back from him toward the door, him following. Then he was in the doorway, his body seeming to block that doorway, even though he isn't all that big. They were on the outside trying to see over his shoulder, looking at me inside the room.

I didn't hear what any of them were saying.

After a minute, Amarius turned his back to them.

Then I saw Ariel's face outside the glass. He was talking to green-coat.

And — oh, no — I didn't want to see Ariel now, I didn't want to hear his voice. Ariel does not lie, so I must not hear what he'll say to me.

I took my fingers out of my ears and stopped humming.

"Excuse me," I said, and the ones outside, they all stared in at me as though a monkey in a zoo had suddenly begun talking.

"I'm going to the ladies' room," I said.

I used my most grown-up voice. I didn't say "bathroom" or "girls' room."

"Down the hall, second door on the left," white-coat said, sticking her head back inside the door. "Someone will show you."

I've been there a dozen times. No one needs to show me. I only said that so they wouldn't wonder where I was going because I wasn't going to the ladies' room.

"I can count," I said. I held up my hand, closed into a fist, then unfolded one finger at a time. "One, two," I said. "And this is my left hand." I smiled and held it up to show her.

I shouldn't have done that, I could tell. All of them looked nervous and turned to each other.

Miss Dearly was out in the hall, talking with Ariel and green-coat.

No one tried to stop me.

I sped down the hall, turned corridors, found the

room they put her in that first day. Isolation. Room number two. They hadn't let me in to see her, but Amarius had helped me sneak down the hall that first day. Except they'd caught us both and stopped us. Grown-ups only, they said. Grown-ups they let in, two minutes at a time, two times an hour.

So why won't they let in her sister?

Because it is hospital rules. No children.

I'm not a child.

They won't stop me this time.

Walk fast, I said to myself. Stand up tall and straight, like they tell us in school. No one will stop you if you know where you're going. If you act like you know, they don't think to stop you.

The nurse's desk was right there outside the door, but there was no nurse sitting there.

My heart was thumping crazily, but I opened the door to room number two.

There was only one bed inside the room.

I went up to the bed.

No!

Her mouth hung open. There were no teeth, only gums showing in that mouth. The hair was white, and so thin it barely covered her head.

"What are you doing here?" I said. "Get out! This is my sister's bed. Where's my sister?"

I grabbed her arm. It was soft, and the flesh slid over the bone.

"Hush! How did you get in here?" Two of them,

dressed in white with masks, they grabbed at my arms. But I was much stronger, and faster, and I twisted away out of the room and down the hall.

There was someone at the nurse's desk now, someone starched and brand-new looking. *Mrs. Rogers,* it said on her little plastic shield.

"Where's Callie?" I asked.

"Callie?"

"My sister. You know, she was here last night. Day before, too."

"Oh. Room number two?" she said.

"Yes. Where is she?"

She looked like she didn't know what to tell me. She looked around, as if looking for help.

"Wait just a minute," she said. "Can you wait a minute?"

Yes.

No.

She left, and I did, too.

Because suddenly I knew where to go. I had heard something, in spite of my humming, had heard that Callie was grave today. Grave, in Intensive Care.

All I had to do was find Intensive Care.

It took a while, but I found it. I knew I would.

Intensive Care. Stop. Do not Enter.

Danger. No Smoking. Oxygen in Use.

There was only one door, a big double one. And there were nurses at the nurses' desk.

I backed up to the elevator door where I could stand and watch.

I would wait till they were gone.

There were big metal tanks — oxygen tanks? — stacked by a wall. A man was taking them on wheeled carts, one at a time, into Intensive Care.

I would walk along beside him, on the opposite side, not the nurse's desk side. No one would notice.

The man would ask, and I'd say, "I'm allowed. Two times each hour, I'm allowed."

Sound like you know the rules, and what can they do?

"For two minutes," I'd say firmly.

And he wouldn't ask anymore.

I waited for my chance.

The three at the desk were laughing.

Can you laugh when Callie is grave? Can you joke? Or don't you really know either?

The man lifted another tank onto his wheeled cart and headed for the door.

I darted out and walked beside him.

At first, he didn't notice that I was there. No one noticed me.

I pushed the door and held it for him.

He nodded. "You goin' in here?"

But I was already in.

Three beds.

A man was in one. Another old woman was in the other. And a tiny bald man, with tubes running from his head and arms and nose in the last.

And that was all.

Where was Callie?

Then I saw her name. It was on a chart on the foot of the bed — the bed with the tiny bald man.

Callie! It was Callie!

It was.

But they had shaved her head, her beautiful hair, from the front, right to the middle of her head. And there were tubes and stuff attached, coming right out of her skull.

Why?

"Callie?"

I looked quickly around. There were nurses, but no one had seen me yet.

"Callie." I took her hand, put my mouth against her ear. "Callie, you're going to get better. You won't be grave anymore. I need you, Callie, I —"

Did I dare? If I said it — would I kill her if I said it?

No. I had to tell her. She needed to know. She really did.

She didn't look as if she could hear me, not as if she could hear anything.

But in that stillness, suddenly, I knew she could hear me. I knew.

How?

"'Cause I know He hears me," I heard Amarius telling me in my mind. "My God, He knows, and I know He hears me."

I knew, too.

Callie could hear.

"I love you," I told her, right into her ear. Then I put

my mouth on hers, breathed out my air into her. "I love you, you know."

She didn't answer, but I knew what she was saying, inside her bald head. I knew what she was saying. She was smiling and saying, "I know."

Chapter 16

I didn't know how long we waited — two days, two weeks, four weeks, four years? No, it only seemed like years, sitting in that glass room waiting for Callie to be better. I waited, and Ariel waited, and Amarius and Miss Dearly waited. Ariel slept there, and then went to work, slept, and then went to work or home to feed Miss Mannie. He and Miss Dearly both came and went because of work. But I stayed all the time, and Amarius stayed with me.

I began to keep track of time by the changes in clothes that Ariel and Miss Dearly brought to me — clean underwear and shirt every day, clean jeans every other day. Four changes of jeans, eight days.

Ariel looked so tired. If there had been any room left in me for worry, I think I would have worried about him the way I worried for Callie. He was so tired; he worked so hard. But at least school was over and he didn't have to do that and work, too.

Callie and I had missed the May Fair, but I couldn't worry about that either. I could hardly think. It was also getting harder and harder to hear. There was so much news that I couldn't hear. I couldn't even hear music playing in my head anymore. And once when I tried to write a song for Callie, it died away before I could capture even one single note.

It was only once in a while, when Amarius would turn to me, touching me lightly on my knee, that I could hear. I knew that he wouldn't say things that I couldn't bear to hear.

We would talk about Callie then, plan our secret trips so I could sneak in and see her. We had managed to get me in to her three times.

She never knew that I was there.

It was the morning of the ninth day, that the two in the gray suits came back. Ariel was with them.

Amarius was beside me on the couch. He jumped up in that fast way he had, and they all moved together, over to the door, away from me.

They didn't have to worry. I couldn't hear. I didn't even have to put my fingers in my ears anymore or hum. I could close my ears without all that.

They stood at the door a very long time while I read a magazine.

There was a picture of a hungry girl in the magazine,

her big eyes looking sad out at me. "You can save her life," the words said under the picture. "Or you can turn the page."

She looked a little like Callie.

I will save your life, I thought. What do I have to do?

Send money.

But we didn't have money. I couldn't even send Mama the money. Her letter was still under my mattress.

After a long while, Amarius came back to my couch, and Ariel was with him.

The gray-suits were out in the hall.

Amarius touched my knee lightly.

Check Ariel's face, Amarius's. Are there tears?

No.

"What?" I said.

Noises flooded in. Metallic sounds, elevators and carts clanking. Soft-soled shoes squeaking, hurrying past in the hall. A voice on a loudspeaker calling for Dr. Heart. Could there really be a Dr. Heart?

"Can you listen?" Amarius asked. "I've got to tell you — it's not the best news. Not the worst, either," he added quickly.

"Callie?"

"Not Callie," Ariel said. "She's the same."

Then what? And why was Amarius bringing me bad news? He never has.

I looked from him to Ariel. Ariel had gotten old. Had we maybe been here years?

No. Eight days, nine. Four pairs of jeans.

“Can you listen?” Amarius said. “Can you hear it all the way through? Good and bad?”

“She can,” Ariel said. He sat down next to me, very close. “Can’t you, Mary Belle?”

Could I? Of course. If it wasn’t about Callie. I’ve never been a coward.

I took a deep breath. “Go on.”

“See?” Ariel said, and he looked out the glass window to the people in the hall. “Them outside?”

“The suits?”

He nodded. “They’re from County Welfare. I guess you know by now that everybody knows. About Mama, I mean.”

It didn’t seem to matter anymore.

I shrugged.

“Problem is,” Ariel went on, “there’s no money for Callie, for the hospital —”

“What?!! What’s that mean?”

He looked up at Amarius.

“It means foster care. For all of us,” he said.

At least his mouth said that, but I didn’t hear the words.

I folded my arms and leaned against the lumpy brown sofa.

“I’ll read my magazine now,” I said, and I turned to the picture of Callie, her hungry eyes looking out at me.

“But you don’t have to be separated,” Amarius said to me, right in my ear. “Maybe.”

You wouldn’t lie to me?

He wouldn't lie to me.

I put the magazine back down. "Then how?" I said.

He and Ariel exchanged looks.

And that's when I knew. Why did it take so long for smart ideas to come to my head?

"You!" I said to Ariel. "You're grown up! You can be the papa!"

He touched my head, just as he had done the day of the picnic.

"I'm only sixteen," he said.

"Almost seventeen."

"Well, yes."

"Then?"

Again he gave Amarius that look.

"Maybe next year," Ariel said, turning back to me. "Meanwhile, it's only for about a year and —"

"No!" I said. "I won't do it! Not a year, not even a week! I'll run away, I'll take Callie and —"

"You're not listening!" Ariel said. "Since it's just over a year till I'm eighteen, the county people said they'll let" — he paused — "they'll let Miss Dearly do it. She worked it out. She knows how to get around the county people. And she wants to do it."

Oh, yes! Lord, yes! Why wasn't I smart enough to think of that? Amarius and Miss Dearly Aikens.

"Miss Dearly?" I said. "Really?"

Ariel nodded.

"Amarius, too?" I asked. I couldn't look at Amarius because suddenly I felt very, very shy.

"No." Ariel shook his head.

"They think I'm too old," Amarius said, that chuckle back in his voice. "They think maybe I'll be meeting the Lord pretty soon. But Miss Dearly, she'll be fine as a mama for a time."

How odd, how very odd. Miss Dearly and Amarius, our new mama and papa — because I knew that no matter what the county people said, Amarius would be part of our family. How very weird.

But then what is it that makes a mama and a papa *be* a mama and a papa, the real kind, that is? What is it that is needed to make the kind of mama and papa that a girl needs, or a boy for that matter? I would think about that, but already I knew one thing: It didn't have anything to do with who borned you.

"Then they won't separate us?" I asked. "Promise?" I looked first at Ariel, then at Amarius.

Amarius rolled his eyes till the whites showed. "Now *how* am I going to promise that?" he asked, his hands on his hips.

I shrugged.

"Okay, Mary Belle?" Ariel asked. He had put his head back against the couch and closed his eyes.

I nodded. "Okay." But I had so many questions. Where would we live? Our house? I felt very shy thinking about living at Amarius's house and didn't think I'd want to do that. But I also knew that I wouldn't ask those questions right now.

I stood up. "Can I tell Callie?"

Ariel just frowned, his eyes still closed.

But Amarius's eyes were shining. I knew what he was thinking: Later, we will find a way in, find a way to see her, after the doctors and the gray-suits are gone.

Yes, later.

Later, I thought, I'll whisper in her ear. I'll sing to her. Callie, you can wake up now, I'll sing. You can get better and we can all go home. And Callie, guess what? We've got ourselves a brand-new papa and mama. And oh, Callie, you'll be surprised at who they are. They are not the kind of papa and mama that will run away from you. They're a different kind, a kind you can count on.

Then I'll breathe my breath into her and I'll say, I love you Callie. And inside her head, she'll say back, I know.

Chapter 17

But that is not at all what happened. No. When Amarius and I went down the hall to Callie's room later on that afternoon, we were not able to sneak me in. There were people everywhere, doctors and nurses hurrying in and out of her room. The speaker was on, calling for Dr. Heart, and as we watched, they rushed a huge machine into her room. They were in there a long while.

Amarius and I, we sat on a stiff wooden bench against a wall. Amarius pinched his pants legs between his fingers.

After a while, all the hurrying stopped, and the doctors and nurses began coming back out. One after the other. They seemed to be drooping, bent and dull, like flowers after a hard rainstorm.

None of them would look our way. Then one of the doctors, a tall one in a green suit, he looked over at us, at Amarius and me on our bench against the wall. The look on his face was puzzled, almost scared, the way a little kid looks when he's broken something. He started toward us, and Amarius got up to meet him, slowly, slowly.

They met in the middle of the hall.

When Amarius turned back to me, he was crying. It was not loud, his crying. But tears rolled down his face and fell from his chin onto his clean white shirt, the one that Miss Dearly had brought to him just that very morning.

The tears made shiny silver tracks, like snails leave across the porch at night.

Oh, do not cry, whatever it is could not be so bad.

No.

Before he could reach my side, I turned and ran out of that place.

Eight, no, nine days, I hadn't been out in the daylight, but I ran out then.

Where? Where do I run?

Home.

No. No home if Callie isn't there.

Ariel is there.

No. Ariel's at work.

Run.

But where?

It doesn't matter. Somewhere.

Run!

I ran, oh, I did, I ran fast. Out of the town, and across

Hairy Bear Mountain.

My legs hurt, my chest hurt, I couldn't breathe.

There was a stitch in my side, and I breathed shallow, tiny breaths like Callie breathed, as if she had been running hard, just like me.

Still, I ran.

It was cold on Hairy Bear Mountain, even though the sun was still shining. When you are up in a mountain so high, why isn't it warmer there, so much closer to the sun?

I heard the truck and knew what it was long before I knew that I knew. It was climbing steadily behind me, shifting gears, spinning pebbles and rocks beneath its wheels. It was coming after me, to get me. To tell me some awful lie.

A truth.

When I realized what it was — Amarius's truck — I darted from the path off into the woods. Big black pickup truck could not cut through woods and underbrush and under trees. Amarius couldn't catch me to tell me why the tears ran down his face and off his chin.

I scrambled low beneath the trees, running bent double, until the truck had lost me.

Still, I kept up the climb, up the mountain. Up, up.

It grew dark, and even colder.

I wasn't running now. My legs ached, and though I told them, Run, run! they didn't obey. I slowed and walked, and then for a while, when I was too tired to walk, I crawled some. Through grass and thickets and brambles I crawled, until I found a cave. Not really a cave. Just a hidden place between some rocks.

The rocks were still warm from the sun, although the sun was long gone. I crawled into the space between the rocks. I wished I had a light, a flashlight. Was I sharing this place with a snake? A snake would like this warmed place. Yes? No? It didn't matter. I didn't want to lie down, to sleep, but my body wouldn't go on anymore.

I would sleep a while, and when my legs were able, I'd go again. I thought I was thirsty, but that's the last thought I had till I opened my eyes again and it was morning.

No. Not morning.

Lights shining somewhere in the woods, headlights. A voice. Ariel.

"Mary Belle? Where are you? Are you here? Can you hear me? Please answer if you can hear me."

Ariel. My brother.

Yes, I'm here, but I can't answer you because I know what you'll tell me. You'll tell me the reason for Amarius's tears.

I held very still, shivering, not letting even a breath escape me.

"Mary Belle? Are you there? Do you hear me? Please answer."

Promise that you won't tell me?

"Mary Belle?"

were gone.

I was alone again. And so cold. I was so cold. My teeth chattered. I wrapped my arms around myself, but I couldn't keep out the cold.

Move. That's what will warm you, move and you won't think.

All through that night I heard that truck, shifting gears, clanking, doors slamming. And I heard a voice other than Ariel's — Amarius with his soft, dark voice, the chuckle in his voice all gone.

It was dark, no moon. So cold.

How do they know that I'm on this mountain?

Run. They're closer now. They've come back. Do they smell me, the way animals smell other animals who are afraid?

I got up and started to run. In the dark, without the moon, it was hard to move, harder still to do it with no sound.

I scrambled up a pebbled cliff, slipped, sending a shower of pebbles falling, falling.

And then suddenly, the truck was there before me, and I was full in its headlights. Like an animal, I was cornered.

"You go away!" I yelled. "Both of you. Go away and leave me alone!"

"Mary Belle!" Ariel yelled.

The truck doors slammed — once, twice. Ariel and Amarius were coming for me.

I turned to run, but they caught me up.

What a howling then. It surprised me so that I stopped struggling for the moment, and then the howling stopped.

Me. It was me howling like that, like a mountain lion, caught up in one of those leg traps.

Oh, do not, do not make sounds like that. You are a girl, not a wild animal.

But I couldn't stop it.

I howled and they held me, one on either side.

I fought, but oh, they were strong, those men. But I was strong, too. I even got them down, tumbled to the ground, but they didn't let me go.

We lay together on the ground, and I fought and scratched, but they held me there. And I wasn't the only one making sounds. They were, too — big gulping sobs from Ariel, a weeping sound from Amarius.

"Mary Belle, I was so scared, I thought I'd lost you, too!" Ariel sobbed to me.

They held me tight between their chests. They cried and cried, but I didn't cry. I didn't cry, but I howled. Like some stupid wild thing, I howled.

Callie. It was for Callie that we carried on. Callie, my sister, Callie, our sister. Callie. Our Callie. She is dead.

Chapter 18

What do you dress a sister in when they're going to put her in a grave, a hole in the ground?

You dress her in a dancing dress, a May Queen's dress. You give her something to take with her, a rag dog for her arms, and you give her a doll, her doll Lisa, to hold her by the hand. And you're grateful, so grateful, that you have finished the hem of her dancing dress.

I didn't want to decide those things. But Ariel and Amarius and Dearly — I called her Dearly now — they made me help them decide. They even made me come with them to pick out a casket. We went to the Loving and Gay Funeral home, and yes, that is really the name of that awful place. We stood around, all of us, looking at those caskets.

"Oh, that one, please, the one with a pink pillow. Can

she have the one with the pink pillow, that is padded all the way around inside?" I asked.

"She's dead, Mary Belle, she can't feel the pillow," Dearly said.

"I know. But please, can she have the pink pillow?"

"Yes."

"Oh, good."

So when that was over, and since we were already in town, we went to Zook's Place, a tiny diner kind of place, where all the farm and mountain people go when they come to town. We ate supper there, all four of us together. That was Dearly's idea. It was a good idea, too. I didn't want to go home.

But after we ate, we had to go home — Dearly and Ariel and Amarius said so, although I would rather have stayed on the mountain again. We went back to our house to sleep. Our house, our room, where Callie's things were all still around — her clothes, her books, those bits of paper where she wrote her lists.

I had to sleep in our room, even though Callie wasn't there. It was the first night in seven years that I'd slept there alone.

But I was not to be alone. Dearly, she said she was going to sleep there, right there in Callie's bed.

"You need someone," she said, "to keep you company."

I do. I need Callie.

But first we had to do some work. We changed the sheets on the beds, and Lord! I was embarrassed. I don't think I'd changed the sheets since Mama left, and I where. But it was all right, because Dearly had brought her own from her house. She had brought fresh sheets, white and ironed, sheets that rustled as we spread them over the beds.

When Dearly pulled Callie's bed away from the wall to get at the mattress, two folded papers fell to the floor. I picked them up — probably more of Callie's lists. I couldn't read them then. I took them back to my side of the room and tucked them in a book beside my bed. I would read them sometime, but not right then.

When we finished Callie's bed, I told Dearly that I wanted to make up my own bed. Mama's letter was still beneath my mattress, and I didn't want to take a chance that Dearly might see it.

I felt scared about that letter — somewhere Mama was waiting for money. And she didn't know that Callie was dead. But I couldn't deal with that, not any of it, so I just left that letter where it was.

While I was changing my bed, Dearly lifted her overnight bag and laid it on Callie's bed. She took out a long white nightdress, two of them, shook them out, and held one up to me.

"Want to take a bath and put this on?" she asked. "It's soft and warm." She held up the other, just like it. "I have two — they're my favorites." She laughed softly. "You know what I do? I wear one when I'm feeling sad. It makes me feel better. It really does."

Oh, yes, I'm feeling sad.

But I hesitated. "It's awfully big," I said.

She laughed.

"No!" I said. "I didn't mean that. I didn't mean that you're big. I just meant —"

"I know what you meant. Would you like to try it?"

I would.

I went in the bathroom. Someone, not me, had cleaned the bathroom and put up clean towels. They weren't towels I'd seen before. They were white, thick and rich and very soft. And there were fresh bars of soap and something sweet smelling in the air.

I took a long, long hot bath, and when I was finished, I felt different, sweet smelling and fresh for the first time in a long time. I hadn't been able to bathe at the hospital. I'd just washed my different parts, arms, legs, feet, one at a time, in the sink.

When I was dried, I put on Dearly's gown. It was much too big for me, long and flowing, with a high neck and long sleeves, and it trailed behind me on the floor. But it was soft feeling, and warm, too, and that was good because even in summer, nights get cold at the foot of the mountains and that night was already cold.

I turned back the sleeves so that my hands would stick out, then clutched the bottom of the gown up so I wouldn't trip.

When I came out of the bathroom, Dearly called from the kitchen. "Mary Belle? We're in here."

I went to the kitchen. Amarius and Ariel were there, sitting one on either side of the table, coffee cups in front of them, a pot of coffee between them. Dearly was at the stove.

But Ariel looked up and

look like an angel in that," he said. "An angel or a waif, or —"

He didn't finish.

"Want something warm, Mary Belle?" Dearly said.

I wasn't hungry, but something warm sounded good.

I nodded, and Dearly brought me a mug of something and put it on the table.

She pulled out a chair for me. "Sit," she said.

I did. I sat, picked up the mug and sniffed. Soup. Chicken soup?

"Drink it," Dearly said. "It's good for you."

She went back to what she was doing at the stove and the sink.

"How you doing?" Ariel asked me.

I shrugged.

"You?" I asked.

"Yeah," he said, and he shrugged, too.

I looked at Amarius. He nodded.

Old. Tired.

Oh, don't get sick, Amarius. Don't get sick, too.

But I couldn't worry about that, not yet.

I just sat, sipping my soup, and Ariel and Amarius, they sat with their coffee, and we were quiet together. It didn't feel too bad.

Dearly, she was moving quietly around the kitchen, talking to herself from time to time. She was stirring something on the stove, unloading grocery bags of food into the refrigerator.

I should tell her, We can do all right. We don't need your help, you know.

But I couldn't say that. Not because I couldn't lie. I couldn't say it because she's smart. She could see.

The three of us kept sitting there, watching Dearly move quietly, efficiently around the kitchen.

Odd to sit here, while someone else does all the work.

Do you think we could have chocolate pudding tomorrow night? And bacon and eggs for breakfast? Could we? And maybe fried chicken tomorrow night? You know how Callie loves . . . well, anyway. And grapes and Mallomars and ice cream? And new jeans for Ariel? And please, do you think I could have a bathrobe, I've always wanted a bathrobe.

Greedy, greedy heart.

Callie was dead. And all I was thinking of was what I wanted.

What I really wanted was Callie back.

What I really couldn't have was Callie back.

But I also couldn't stop all the wanting that came to my head.

I drank my soup, and after a while, I felt very sleepy. Clean and warm and dry. And sleepy.

I got up and took my mug to the sink to rinse it out, but Dearly took it from my hands. "To bed," she said. "Tomorrow's a hard day. To bed, and I'll do this."

Thank you. Thank you for doing this, for doing all of this.

For some reason, I couldn't say that, though. I

they called after me as I went to our room.

"'Night, Mary Belle," Ariel said.

"'Night," Amarius said. "Sleep sweet."

I nodded because it was all I could do.

I went in my room and turned on the light.

I got into bed, propped up the pillow, picked up my book, opened it, and took out Callie's notes.

Two notes.

I opened the first.

This is what it said:

> These are my favrit foods:
> marshmelows
> peanut butter
> choclat ice cream
> turkey
> frid chicken
> Hot dogs
> caviar

Caviar? That liar! She had never tasted caviar in her whole entire life. She had probably read that somewhere in a book. She had even spelled it right, so that proved it.

I unfolded the other paper — another list.

Oh, Lord.

"My sister," it said. "My sister is . . ."

What if she knew how much I hated cooking and

making her lunch and taking care of her and everybody and —

I wanted not to read that list, yet I was reading it before I could stop myself, reading it, my heart pounding.

> My sister is Mary Belle.
> She is smart.
> She is prety.
> She is our boss now.
> She does not like to boss me. She just has to.
> She is sad somtimes.
> She hates Miss Mannie.
> She hates to dance.
> She makes up prety songs.
> She is my best friend.
> That's all.

That's all?

Oh, Callie!

My sister is smart.

Not really, Callie. If I was smart, I would have taken better care of you.

My sister does not like to boss me. She just has to.

But you said I did, Callie! Remember that day when you said I was happy Mama was gone because I just like to boss you around? Are you taking it back now? You are, aren't you?

My sister hates Miss Mannie.

don't love her the way you do.

My sister is my best friend.

Yes. And my sister is my best friend. But my sister is dead.

That's when I started to cry. I cried and cried for a long time, trying to be quiet. Ariel must have heard, though, because he came in, and he sat on my bed and rubbed my back.

"I know, I know," he kept saying softly, over and over again. "I know, honey."

Honey??

Oh, do not, do not talk like that because I'll cry forever. I cried so hard that I got the hiccups, and he went and got me water.

I heard him in the kitchen, getting water, talking to Amarius and Dearly.

He said something, but I didn't hear his words.

"She needed to cry something awful," Amarius answered. "She'll be better now."

I do, oh, I do.

Will I really be better, Amarius? Will I, Ariel?

Promise? Promise if you can.

Chapter 19

Next morning I woke up early, feeling very, very scared. We were going to have a funeral and put Callie in a grave, and then she would be really gone. And what about Mama? She'll be awful mad if she comes back and Callie's gone. Should I take out the letter, write to her at that address? Should I tell her what happened?

Mama, I'll say, I didn't take good enough care, and Callie is dead now.

I was lying there, wondering those things, when I noticed that Dearly was watching me from Callie's bed.

"What're you thinking about, sweet child?" she asked softly, a little lilt in her voice, like an almost-laugh.

"About Mama. She'll be so mad."

"Mad?"

"I didn't take good enough care of Callie."

For a long time she didn't answer, and I thought she

mama didn't take good care of Callie, Mary Belle. Your
mama didn't take good care of any of you children."

Dearly was quiet a while and then spoke again. "We tried to reach your mama, Mary Belle, before Callie died. But —"

But you don't know where she is. And I have an address for her right under my mattress, right here, I'm lying on it, and Lord, I feel so guilty.

"Mary Belle," Dearly said, and she turned her head on the pillow to face me from across the room. "You have to know this. We know where your mama is."

"What?" I sat straight up. "Where?"

How? Had she seen my letter? Had she looked under my mattress?

Dearly sat up, too, swinging her long legs over the side of the bed, then got up and came over to sit beside me on my bed.

"Your mama," Dearly said, "has a friend in town. You know Corley, don't you? We figured Corley might know, and he did. He called your mama and —"

"Called her? Where is she? When's she coming back? Does she know about . . . Callie?"

"She knows."

"She knows?"

Oh, and she must be so mad.

"Yes. We told her."

"Is she coming home now? Did she ask about . . . anything else?"

Dearly took both my hands inside of hers, cupping

hers tightly around mine, making a little cage from which my hands, like birds, could not escape.

"She's not coming back," Dearly said, still holding my hands so tightly.

"Not coming? Why?"

"Mary Belle, she's sorry about Callie, I know. But she says there's nothing she can do about it now, and even if she'd been here, she says, she couldn't have done anything. So she's not coming home, not for the funeral, not for anything, not ever, she says. She's got a job now, dancing. I'm sorry." Dearly was watching me closely. "She asked for you, you especially, Mary Belle," Dearly went on. "She said to tell you to keep on with that music you write."

"Mama said that?"

Dearly nodded. "Yes. And she said —"

"What?"

Dearly sighed. "She said that life is hard. She said it as if it explained something. 'Tell Mary Belle life is hard,' she said. 'Life is sad and life is hard.'"

Yes, oh, Lord, yes. And people like Mama, they make it hard. For everyone, they make it hard.

Dearly stared at our hands, then released mine slowly and began rubbing my wrists, as though to bring back the circulation, as though she knew she had been holding too tight. "Mary Belle," she said. "It's not that she doesn't love you. That's not the reason that she won't come back. You have to believe that. It's just that —"

"What?"

She kept on rubbing my wrists. For a long, long time,

said, almost in a whisper, "I don't know. I swear to God, I don't."

I don't know either, except that I know suddenly that she is an unnatural mama. I have read of such things in books. Mama is like Amarius said she is — a wild animal, a wolf, leaving us as if we were a bunch of wild pups.

And it's weird, but I still wished that I had money to send her for a dancing dress.

So then we got up and dressed and had our breakfast. Dearly made us scrapple and eggs and she paid special attention to the way I like my eggs cooked, the yellow still soft but the white not all wet and slimy. She put a cover on the fry pan to keep them that way.

Then we went to church. We had a funeral in Amarius's church, his and Dearly's. I was surprised to know that Dearly was a minister, just like a man. I didn't know that women could do that, too. But I guess it's not so strange that I didn't know that. I knew nothing at all about church, seeing as how I'd hardly ever been inside of one.

This church, though — this church was nice. It was small and plain, and it smelled nice, like clean people, not all hot and sweaty, and it smelled of the heat outside, and something else that I couldn't put my finger right on, but something sweet, maybe like babies or talcum powder. The altar place was small and bare, and the chairs for the ministers were just plain old folding chairs. There were long black benches for us to sit on. There were no big statues and no fancy flowers or curtains, not at all like I'd have thought. And in the middle of the aisle, that long silver box that I couldn't take my eyes off.

The church was crowded with people by the time we got there. People from town I saw, like Ella Mae Rooks and her daughter and identical twin, Ellie Mae Rooks, and some of the teachers, too. Callie's teacher, Miss Callahan, was there. Even though it was already summer and school was out, a lot of the children from the third grade were there, too. And then I had the weirdest thought — that if I turned around real quick, I'd see Mama standing in the back of the church. But, of course, I wouldn't.

Walking down that aisle between Ariel and Amarius, I felt suddenly shy, so many faces looking hard at us as if we were in a wedding or something. This isn't a show, I wanted to say to them.

But then the service began, and oh! that music! There was an organ, and a choir made up of lots of children, a choir full of children singing for Callie. The children were all from Dearly's and Amarius's church, some of them the same ones that were in Callie's class. Naomi Lynn was one of them.

And oh, Callie, I wished you were here — because after they sang, you know what they did? They danced, they danced for you!

See, this is what happened. The choir was right in the front, and after they sang, they took off their singing robes and put on these colored robes, with all different and they swayed and danced, wearing the long robes with the bright colors. I do wish you could have seen them — they were so beautiful, swaying and clapping like that. They weren't afraid to come near your silver box either. Each of them waved to it, as though they were waving good-bye to you. That was the title of the dance, the lady said — "Godspeed" — God speed you on your way.

I didn't know you could give a name to a dance the way I give names to my songs. And Callie, I wish so much I had a piano — a guitar — anything. I would write a song for you, a song that would go with their dancing. I wouldn't call it what they did, though. I'd give it a different name, wouldn't speed you on your way.

Amarius sat on one side of me, his head moving to the rhythm of the music.

Ariel sat on the other side, holding my hand so tightly, all the way through the service he did. Everybody was crying. Amarius cried, Ariel did, and I did, too. Even some of the dancers did, although they kept right on dancing. Naomi Lynn was crying, Callie. Naomi Lynn was May Queen in your place, Callie. I knew that would make you happy, that you'd like to know that. Toward the end, Ariel put his arm around my shoulders, squeezing me tight. "Callie must love this," he said through his tears. Funny, but he was smiling.

You mean you think she *can* see us?

I ask myself that. Can she?

I don't know, but Ariel, he knows.

When the children were finished, Dearly said a final prayer, a poem, more like. It was said so pretty, it made me sit up and listen, and wish that I could hear it again. I'll ask her to write it down for me, and maybe someday I can set it to music.

It went something like this:

Lord, you have sent this child out to us,
Lent her to us.
A creature to gambol and dance on your plains
a while.
But now is gone.
Our heart remains
at your service.
But oh, we weep: too short her time with us.
Unfair, we whisper in our sleep.

Sleep on. And heal. And spend your rage
for she has found her place.
'Tis not apart.
Awake, come spring,
and find her small and safe,
and sleeping in your heart.

We all went outside then in the hot summer sun, right outside the church, and they buried Callie in the churchyard.

Yes, she's dead. Yes, I can even say the word, at least in my head I can say it. But they don't have to have that burial thing, with everyone looking on, taking a look at the casket and at Ariel and me, while they put her in the ground.

Go away, all of you.

I turned away myself. I'd come back here another time, alone, when all the rest were gone. Then I'd deal with this.

I turned my back, and then it was over and we headed back home.

The four of us walked together, Ariel still holding my hand.

Dearly took off her minister robe, and she walked on the outside, next to Amarius.

It was a long, hot walk, but we had decided against a car, and it was good that we had. The walk was doing me good.

We came up the old rutted path over the hill, and the house came into view, all clustered round with trees. Some awful things had happened there, but happy things, too, and Lord, I loved that place — the trees, the woods and fields, the deer, our house, the mountain that hung over all, watching. Our windows had been opened wide that morning, and the smell of the scrapple that Dearly had cooked still lingered in the air.

And how can I love the smell of scrapple when Callie, my Callie, is dead?

I do not know. But I know I do.

I thought of the fresh towels in the bathroom, the clean white sheets on my bed, and suddenly, I wanted so bad to go back to bed, to sleep for a long, long time.

No, I'm not running away. I know all about Callie. But for now I need to sleep, for I am very, very tired.

Chapter 20

Summer has come and gone, and it is almost fall now, three whole months without Callie. The trees have changed color, are red and gold and brown and even pink. There is one, my favorite, still summer green, with a fire-red patch in its side. There is a small one, a baby oak, that is all brown, not really very pretty, but for one branch that is almost pure gold. Callie would have liked that tree.

We still live in our house all week, with Dearly sleeping now in Mama's room. And Amarius, while the weather is still nice, sleeps on a sofa on the porch. On weekends, we move back to Amarius's and Dearly's house. Ariel and I, we each have a tiny room there in a loft above the living room.

Moving there on weekends is partly for Amarius's and Dearly's comfort, but partly for me so that I can practice on their piano. I practice there every day for an hour or so, but on the weekends, I practice four and five hours each day. Amarius and Dearly tell me my job is to learn the piano, to learn music as good as anything. They laugh: you'll be a concert pianist someday, they say.

But I won't be a concert pianist — I know that. I'm good, but I'm not that good. That's not why I'm at the piano. No, I write music at the piano, because when I'm at the piano for hours and hours, it's as if I'm not really there anymore, as if the music has taken me away. Though of course I know better.

But Mama, when she heard music, in her head or anywhere, she *had* to dance, *had* to move, had to *go* with the music. Until finally one day, she just danced away. And I think that maybe she couldn't help that.

Funny, but thinking about music makes me think of Amarius, and Ariel, too. Amarius and Ariel, they're both so sure about their God. Maybe God and music are one. I do not know.

But I do know one thing — I know that although life is hard and sad, sad for all of us, it's not always sad. I could tell Mama that. I think it isn't something that she knows, that life isn't always hard and sad. She should know that our garden is wonderfully rich now. There are beans and corn and snap peas and flowers, and we spend hours on the porch, shelling peas and limas and telling each other stories. And sometimes this summer, Anna Tilley came out to play with me, and Naomi Lynn came, and Amarius's and Dearly's friends came, too.

too. We tell stories and tell tales about each other and tease each other some. Some nights, when we're at their house or at our house, we sit on the porch and talk all night long, till the stars are gone and the sun is coming up, the sky pale and light, with just the morning star hanging there, as if it were reluctant to be gone for another day.

We tell sad stories sometimes, about what it's like to be us. And when we feel good, we tell happier stories about us. And we talk about Callie lots. We talk about what she did and said, and what she was like, and we tell funny stories about her and all the lists of things she used to write. When we talk of Callie, I do most of the talking and they do most of the listening. I guess that's because I have the most to say.

Some nights, when the stars are almost gone, and the morning is creeping up, and Ariel and Amarius and Dearly, they are dozing in their chairs or on the steps, then I talk directly to Callie. I tell her all about what it is like to be here without her. I tell her about the fresh, white sheets, and soap in the bathroom and fruit every day, and that I don't worry about money anymore. I tell her that Miss Mannie is being better fed than ever, that Miss Mannie is getting fat, in fact. And I tell her just about everything about how we're doing.

Better, I tell her, much, much better. Life isn't sad always, and it's not hard always either. Sometimes Callie, it's so much better. Especially now it's happier, with Mama gone — yes, with Mama gone — and Ariel and Amarius and Dearly here, all of us like a family.

Callie, it's better, and hardly anything is missing from our life right now. Hardly anything. But you.

Oh, Callie — I miss you so!